PRAISE FOR THE COUNTRY CLUB MURDERS

"A sparkling comedy of errors tucked inside a clever mystery. I loved it!"
– Susan M. Boyer, *USA Today* Bestselling Author of *Lowcountry Book Club*

"Readers who enjoy the novels of Susan Isaacs will love this series that blends a strong mystery with the demands of living in an exclusive society."
– *Kings River Life Magazine*

"From the first page to the last, Julie's mysteries grab the reader and don't let up."
– Sally Berneathy, *USA Today* Bestselling Author of *The Ex Who Saw a Ghost*

"This book is fun! F-U-N Fun!...A delightful pleasure to read. I didn't want to put it down...Highly recommend."
– *Mysteries, etc.*

"Set in Kansas City, Missouri, in 1974, this cozy mystery effectively recreates the era through the details of down-to-earth Ellison's everyday life."
– *Booklist*

"Mulhern's lively, witty sequel to *The Deep End* finds Kansas City, Mo., socialite Ellison Russell reluctantly attending a high school football game...Cozy fans will eagerly await Ellison's further adventures."
– *Publishers Weekly*

"There's no way a lover of suspense could turn this book down because it's that much fun."
– *Suspense Magazine*

"Cleverly written with sharp wit and all the twists and turns of the best '70s primetime drama, Mulhern nails the fierce fraught mother-daughter relationship, fearlessly tackles what hides behind the Country Club façade, and serves up justice in bombshell fashion. A truly satisfying slightly twisted cozy."
– Gretchen Archer, *USA Today* Bestselling Author of *Double Knot*

"Part mystery, part women's fiction, part poetry, Mulhern's debut, *The Deep End*, will draw you in with the first sentence and entrance you until the last. An engaging whodunit that kept me guessing until the end!"
– Tracy Weber, Author of the Downward Dog Mysteries

"The plot is well-structured and the characters drawn with a deft hand. Setting the story in the mid-1970s is an inspired touch...A fine start to this mystery series, one that is highly recommended."

BIG SHOT

JULIE MULHERN

J & M PRESS

CHAPTER ONE

July, 1975
Miami County, Kansas

*E*legant hands clutched the 12-gauge shotgun. Elegant as in manicured and soft with long fingers. Those hands didn't dig ditches or saw wood or even mow the lawn. Thatcher Cooke had no reason to dig or saw, and he had a teenage boy from down the street mow.

He was dressed for a day at the country club, not the Fin and Feather (also a club, but one dedicated to hunting, fishing, and horseback riding). He grinned at Graham Landingham, puffed his chest, and settled the gun's butt against his shoulder. "Pull!"

He shifted the gun's barrel too quickly.

Bang!

Thatch's shot went wide, and an intact clay pigeon crashed to the earth.

Graham flashed a grin that flirted with smirking. With his madras shorts, golf shirt, and deck shoes, Graham looked as out of place as Thatch. "Nice shooting."

We were at the club's skeet range, in essence an enormous

field. No doubt filled with bugs (bad), rodents (worse) and snakes (worst). I wore khaki pants, a long-sleeved denim shirt, and sturdy boots (in case the snakes left the field for the stations arc). It was too hot for long sleeves, long pants, or the long pauses between Thatch's shots, and my temper was short. I'd come to shoot, not insult other people's talents, or lack thereof.

"You could do better?" Thatch demanded.

Graham chuckled. "I couldn't do worse."

I swallowed an annoyed sigh. Friday afternoon, and the weekend was already off to a rocky start. I'd sensed this weekend was a bad idea. Too many men with outsized egos. Throw in guns and alcohol, July heat, hunting cabins not meant to house people in high summer, cicadas loud enough to make shotgun blasts seem quiet, and my propensity for finding bodies, and the whole thing spelled disaster. In capital letters.

Thatch scowled and reloaded. "Pull!"

The clay pigeon flew across the field. Thatch fired. And missed. Again.

"You do know you're supposed to hit the clay?"

Mocking a man with a shotgun? I frowned at Graham.

The decision to come to the shooting range was a mistake. I could be on a shaded dock with the other woman who'd been corralled into this weekend. I could be enjoying the breeze off the lake (a generous description for the extra-large pond) while I enjoyed a gin and tonic. But no. I'd chosen guns and the opportunity to test my skills, and now I stood in late afternoon sun hot enough to melt the polish off my nails and listened to two men take potshots at each other. Potshots more accurate than their actual shooting.

"Just kicking off the rust," Thatch ground out. "I haven't held a shotgun in months."

"That's your story?" Graham produced another grin.

Thatch's shoulders tightened, a posture that wouldn't help his aim.

I held my tongue. Thatch wouldn't appreciate shooting tips from a woman. Even if I could tell him exactly what he was doing wrong.

As a girl who adored her daddy, I'd embraced his passions—hunting and golf. I learned early how to shoot a gun and swing a club. And because (according to Mother) anything worth doing was worth doing well, I'd excelled.

When I refused to shoot animals, Daddy had introduced me to skeet. We'd spent countless Saturday afternoons blowing apart clay pigeons.

One of Daddy's first lessons? Hold a shotgun like a baby bird.

Thatch gripped his gun as if it were a baseball bat signed by the Royals' third baseman he and Graham had discussed before the shooting began. His death grip coupled with the tightness in his shoulders meant he'd be lucky to hit the broadside of a barn. "Pull!"

Bang!

Thatch wasn't lucky, and Graham laughed out loud when the shot went wide.

"May I try?" Intervening seemed like the best way to avert a murder before cocktail hour.

Thatch forgot his ire, and Graham forgot his mockery. Instead, they stared at me as if my presence surprised them. That or they didn't believe women could shoot skeet. Either way, they'd been so invested in measuring their...egos, they'd forgotten me.

A cocktail on the dock was sounding better and better.

I ignored the 12-gauge double-barrel that Thatch held out. Maybe he thought a 12-gauge was manly, but I could live without the kick. Instead, I claimed a .410 from the gun rack. Then I loaded, stepped forward to station one, and settled the butt against my shoulder.

"You should adjust your stance," said Thatch. "Open up."

Because he was so good at hitting the clays? My stance was fine. "I think I'll stick with what I know."

He grunted his disapproval.

Graham studied me with narrowed eyes. "You need a tighter hold on the fore stock."

For the love of Pete. I forced a small smile, acknowledged his unsolicited advice with a quick nod, and kept my Daddy-approved, firm-but-not-so-tight-I'd-kill-a-baby-bird grip. "Pull!"

I sighted the target and pulled the trigger.

Bang!

The clay pigeon exploded in a satisfying cloud of dust.

"Pull."

This time, the pigeon came from the low house.

I pulled the trigger, reduced the clay to rubble, and reloaded. "Pull."

Two clays. One from the high house and one from the low. I hit them both.

"Where did you learn to shoot? And can Thatcher get lessons?"

"My father taught me." I reloaded and shifted to station two. "Pull."

I hit another clay.

"Nice." Thatch fisted his hands as if the compliment cost him.

"Thank you."

"Does your husband shoot?" Thatch asked. "Skeet, I mean."

My husband was a homicide detective and carried a hand-gun. "He does." We'd discussed skeet after Libba strong-armed us—me, I strong-armed Anarchy—into accepting the invitation to come this weekend. "Pull."

I aimed, and another low-house clay exploded.

Thatch rubbed his chin. "Is he as good as you?" Perhaps he planned on asking Anarchy for shooting tips.

"We'll have to find out." I kept my voice mild. "Pull."

Again, clays flew from the high and low houses.

I shot them both, and, for a half-second, a smirk claimed my lips. I quickly replaced said smirk with a polite smile. "Graham, would you like a turn?"

Graham grimaced. "You're a hard act to follow. Please finish."

I visited all eight stations and didn't miss a single clay, then Graham claimed the gun Thatcher had used, positioned himself at station one, and rested the shotgun's butt against his shoulder. "Pull."

He missed.

Thatcher chuckled.

"Pull!"

Graham missed a second time.

Thatcher crossed his arms and rocked back on his heels. Now he was the one smirking. "Shall we make this interesting?"

Betting? Neither of them had hit a clay yet. I sealed my lips (they wouldn't appreciate my observation) and batted away a determined mosquito.

"Twenty dollars a clay?" asked Thatcher.

"Fifty," Graham replied.

"Let's make it a hundred."

Graham grunted his approval.

"What are the rules?" I asked. "You pay for misses or hits?"

They both turned their scowls my way.

Even though I'd asked a legitimate question, I held up my hands. "Can I get in on this?"

The sun had turned the back of Graham's neck lobster red, he rubbed at his burned skin. "You're not part of the bet, Ellison."

Because I could actually hit the targets?

"To twenty-five?" Graham meant twenty-five clays.

"You can afford to lose that much?" asked Thatch.

Graham produced another smirk. "You haven't hit anything yet."

Neither of them had. Again, I kept that thought to myself. Instead I eyed the field, now filled with their missed clays.

Graham reloaded and lifted the gun to his shoulder.

The cicadas in the distant trees droned louder than ever.

Sweat trickled down my back, but I shivered. Shivered? Why did my shoulders feel as if an icy finger had just tapped for my attention? Dread gripped my spine. Something awful was coming. I was sure of it.

Thatch frowned at me. "You okay, Ellison?"

"Fine. A goose walked over my grave." If I explained my premonition to Thatch or Graham, really to any man but Anarchy, they'd pat my hand and tell me I was being silly. Or emotional. Or both. Few men had faith in women's intuition. Their mistake.

"Pull."

Graham clipped his clay, and he flashed Thatch a wily grin. "That's a hundred to me."

Had Graham missed his early shots on purpose? The sense of dread was near stifling, and I crossed my arms over my chest. I had so much to lose, I couldn't help but shudder.

Anarchy and I were housed in the second to last of six log cabins. Each had a tiny front porch and a screened porch off the back. Each stood in a clearing surrounded by shade trees.

Mother would call the tiny cabin primitive. And she'd be right.

A braided rag rug covered the knotty pine floors. There was also a bed, a dresser, two chairs pushed in at a scarred oak table, a tiny kitchenette, a tinier bathroom, and a window unit air conditioner that made enough noise to drown out a full-scale military operation.

My best friend Libba, who'd joined me for a cocktail, frowned at the offending unit. "I can't hear myself think."

"I can turn it off, but the temperature in here will be stifling within twenty minutes."

She glanced at her watch. "We're due at dinner soon. Turn it off."

I stood and jabbed the unit's red button. The resulting silence was deafening. At least to me.

Libba breathed a relieved sigh. "How will you sleep with that thing running? Oh, wait. Newlyweds." She waggled her brows suggestively. "You don't sleep."

I rolled my eyes at her.

"When will your new husband be here?" she asked.

Anarchy was wrapping up a case and hadn't been able to leave work until late in the day. Instead of having me wait for him, he'd insisted Libba and I make the drive together. "I'm not sure."

"How was shooting?"

"Thatch and Graham were..." I searched for the right word.

"Swaggering?"

"Yes."

"Competitive?"

"They bet a hundred per clay."

She barked a laugh. "How did that work out?"

"Thatch hustled Graham, and Graham hustled Thatch. They morphed from men who couldn't hit a thing to half-decent shots. I watched them."

"How many did they hit?"

"Thirteen each."

"So, a wash?"

"Yes." Should I tell her about my sense of foreboding? Libba would not pat my hand or call me silly. Instead, she'd worry.

There was no reason to ruin her weekend over a feeling. I clinked the ice cubes melting in my gin and tonic and stared at the rag rug.

"How many did you hit?"

I looked up from my study of the rug. "I wasn't part of the bet."

"How many?"

"I didn't miss with the .410 or the 20-gauge."

She grinned. "I bet they loved that."

"They seemed more interested in jabbing at each other than the number of clays I hit."

She rolled her eyes. "Well, duh."

"Why, duh?"

"Thatch is managing partner at their law firm. Has been for several years. Now Graham has thrown his name in the hat for the position." Libba stood and studied her reflection in the tiny mirror above the dresser. "From what I hear, he has a good chance of unseating Thatch."

Now, those potshots made sense.

"Also…"

I waited for more.

Libba's lips curled into an evil smile. "Jinx told me Willa Cooke and Graham were spotted having drinks." Jinx, our dear friend, was a world-class gossip. She was also unfailingly accurate.

"Where?" The answer mattered. The club or one of the restaurants frequented by our set could be entirely innocent. A hotel bar? Not so much.

"Nabil's."

"No one would plan an illicit rendez-vous at Nabil's." Nor could I imagine Thatch's wife, who was willowy and graceful and vague, having enough guile to carry on an affair.

"Maybe they were trying to trick people into thinking their rendez-vous was innocent."

I stared at her as if she'd lost her mind. "Why not be sneaky?" There were plenty of places a couple could go without being spotted. Nabil's wasn't one of them. I'd never darkened its doors without seeing a handful of people I knew.

"Maybe Willa picked the place. She's not sneaky." Libba had that right.

Throw cheating spouses into the weekend's mix and we were guaranteed disaster. The icy finger poked at me again. I squared my shoulders. "Here's a question for you."

Libba lifted her brows and twisted so she could admire the reflection of her near bare back.

"Why does Graham want to be the managing partner? It's not as if he'll make more money. If anything, the time he spends managing the firm means he'll bill fewer hours."

Libba turned toward the mirror and patted a stray hair into place. "Are you serious?"

As serious as a heart attack. Or a shotgun blast. "Yes."

"Ego. Prestige. Bragging rights." Fair points. Especially when it came to Thatch. I remembered Graham's smirk. Those points applied to him as well.

Now I could add professional rivalry to all the reasons this weekend was a bad idea. "Remind me again why we're here."

"Because Charlie and Perry Brandt are old friends."

"That explains why Charlie's here."

"Charlie asked me to come."

"That explains you. Why am I here?"

"You're here to support your best friend." When she'd heard Anarchy and I had been invited, she'd begged me—us—to join her and Charlies on this back-country weekend.

"Liz is here."

"Liz does everything well and looks gorgeous doing it."

"And I don't?" I didn't.

Libba stared at her glass as if she were puzzled where the gin went. "You might shoot well and ride well, but you're not intimidating. You spill things, and you find bodies."

I frowned at her.

She held up her free hand. "You don't judge me. Except for Liz, the women who are here this weekend treat me like I have the plague."

My gorgeous best friend went through boyfriends faster that I went through coffee. She had a zest for living that caught men's eyes—not that she'd knowingly dip her toe into adultery. That didn't stop wives, who'd been thickened by childbirth and aged by surly teenagers, from being nervous.

In addition to Thatch's wife, Willa, and Liz, Melanie Paige was coming. If she'd arrived earlier, Mel would have been at the range with Thatch and Graham and me. The woman was a crack shot.

Then there was Buffy Geller. Her husband Bill had a wandering eye. Buffy didn't trust any woman around him. Or to be more precise, she didn't trust him around other women— especially unmarried women.

As for Merit Dodson, who knew if she worried about Libba? I doubted it. But I could be wrong. Merit was one of those women who believed Eleanor Roosevelt when she said, "Great minds discuss ideas. Average minds discuss events. Small minds discuss people." Using that logic, Libba and I had average to small minds. Merit had little use for us.

Finally there was Graham's wife, Sumner. She'd been beautiful as a girl, but her looks had faded with the passing years. Not that she was going gentle into middle age. She tended to wear clothes too young for her and was the only woman I knew who wore false eyelashes on a daily basis.

Oh, dear Lord.

My inner voice was beginning to sound as judgmental as Mother's.

Who was I to judge if hairy spiders perched above Sumner's

eyes? I bet she thought the short, sometimes-I-forgot-mascara lashes around my eyes were dull as dishwater.

"Aside from Buffy, I don't see any of the women here treating you like a deadly illness. Besides, you're with Charlie now."

Libba might not admit it to herself, to Charlie, or to me, but she'd fallen hard for my high-school flame and current next-door neighbor. She gave a sharp shake of her head. "I needed you here."

"Well, here I am."

She joined me on the edge of the bed and squeezed my hand. "And I'm grateful. Thank you for coming." Extra wetness swam in Libba's eyes and she sniffed.

How many gin and tonics had she drunk on that dock without me? Gin made her weepy. There was no other explanation for the threatening tears. We needed a new subject. Quickly. "What does Perry think of the managing-partner tiff?" Perry, Thatch, and Graham were partners in the same firm.

She snorted. "You'll have to ask him."

I narrowed my eyes. "What do you know?"

"Nothing." She spoke too quickly and studied her watch with more attention than the time deserved. "Charlie promised he'd be here by six. Shall we walk up to the parking lot and meet him?"

What wasn't she telling me? I could badger her. Or I could ask Liz. One option promised aggravation, the other did not. I let Libba's avoidance stand. "Let me turn on the air, then we can go." I rose from my spot on the bed and pressed a button.

The window unit roared to life. Jet engines were quieter. "Ready."

"You're wearing that?" Libba frowned her disapproval.

I frowned back. I'd kept quiet about her halter dress's scandalously deep vee, its color, and its lurid pattern (purple, blue and green paisleys). How dare she question the peasant skirt I'd paired with a scoop neck tee-shirt and cowboy boots? "I am."

"Okay, Annie Oakley."

"You say that now, but if we see a snake, you'll regret those sandals."

"We won't see any snakes. They avoid people. Now, come on." Libba tugged my elbow and held up her empty glass. "We can stop by my cabin for refills on our way."

We stepped outside.

"Ellison," called Sumner. She and Graham had the cabin next to ours. "How was shooting?"

I turned toward the last cabin in the row, and Sumner smiled at us. Like Libba she held an empty old-fashioned.

"Shooting was fine." I couldn't exactly tell her that Graham and Thatch had taunted each other like children on a playground. "But it was hot, I came back thirsty."

Libba lifted her empty glass. "We need more gin, and Ellison forgot her bottle. She was drinking water when I arrived at her cabin."

Sumner stared owlishly, as if Libba had imparted deep wisdom. "One can't travel without gin. And you—" she pointed at me "—need to catch up."

"Catch up with Libba?" I scoffed. "Libba could drink our husbands under the table."

Libba preened as if her hollow leg was a point of pride.

Sumner giggled. And tilted.

Only Graham's sudden appearance and his grip on his wife's arm kept her from falling. He offered me a wry smile. "Seems as if we missed quite a party at the dock."

"So I see."

Sumner hiccupped. "The dock was fun. Sometimes a woman needs to let loose." She pulled free of her husband's grasp. "I am woman. Hear me roar."

Neither her light-pink linen shift (embroidered with

dancing shrimp), nor the blurriness in her baby blue eyes spoke of strength or roaring.

"Rahhr!" Sumner curled her free hand until her fingers looked like claws.

We waved our goodbyes and walked toward Libba's cabin and her stash of gin.

"Tonight should be a hoot," Libba deadpanned.

Inwardly, I cringed. I could be at home with my new husband, curled on the couch watching television, cooled by an air conditioner that didn't sound like a take-off at Cape Canaveral, with nary a hint of doom in sight. Instead… "If this ends in disaster, I blame you."

"Oh, please." Libba rolled her eyes. "What could possibly go wrong?"

CHAPTER TWO

*L*iz and Willa, who'd organized this weekend, had hired a caterer to handle our meals. Because, as Liz wisely pointed out, it wasn't a weekend getaway if she couldn't get away from fixing breakfast, lunch and dinner.

Instead, the woman who regularly catered events at their husbands' law firm had arrived with a van full of food and a handful of helpers.

Those helpers had strung fairy lights in the gazebo near the lake and covered a long picnic table with a blue and white gingham cloth.

Fiesta ware platters filled with cold fried chicken and grilled corn on the cob covered the table. They were joined by bowls of potato salad, baked beans, coleslaw, and sliced cucumbers, tomatoes and onions floating in vinegar water.

Daisies and Queen Anne's lace in mason jars dotted the center of table.

A second table, also covered with a gingham cloth, held enough gin to souse half the British navy, bottles of tonic water, fresh-sliced limes, and a pitcher of lemonade. White wine and beer cooled in a galvanized tub.

Citronella candles' sharp scent perfumed the air. Whether the citrusy odor prevented mosquitos from biting was debatable. I'd hedged my bets and wore OFF rather than perfume.

Charlie and Anarchy sat at the far end of the picnic table with Perry and Tommy. Occasionally, I caught a few words of their conversation. They were discussing lures.

Fishing.

I'd rather watch paint dry. Literally.

I'd brought an easel, tubes of acrylics, and a selection of paintbrushes, and planned on getting up early with Anarchy. Not to fish, but to paint. Maybe I'd go to the lake and watch as my husband cast a line, then I'd paint the morning mist rising from the water.

For now, I sat between Willa and Sumner. If the two women were aware their spouses were vying for the same job, they hid it well. They'd been unfailingly polite.

Buffy sat next to Sumner, and the two women exchanged cool pleasantries. Golf handicaps. Tennis league gossip. The lovely post-swim-team lull in volunteer commitments.

Willa surveyed the table, making sure that everything was up to snuff.

Mel, Libba, Liz and Merit sat across from us.

"Do you remember when we were twelve and went to dances?" Libba swirled the liquor in her glass and glanced at the men at the far end of the table.

Where was she going with this? If she told the story of our first dance, about me throwing up on Billy Fitzhugh when he tried to kiss me, I'd sneak into her cabin, steal her gin, and hide it so well she'd never find it.

"The boys sat on one side of the room, the girls on the other." Her gaze settled on Charlie. "Nothing has changed."

"I disagree," said Mel.

Libba gave her gin and lemonade another swirl. "Oh?"

"Back then, boys were exotic creatures, and we wanted them to cross the room to our side. Now, we know better."

Libba, who knew a great deal about males crossing the room, lifted her brows.

Merit covered a yawn with her palm. Was she tired, or did she find being surrounded by small minds hopelessly boring?

Mel rested her elbows on the table and laced her fingers together. "It's not as if I care about baseball stats or fishing or their investment clubs. Lord knows we can't discuss politics in polite company."

"Or religion," said Libba.

"Please, no one bring up the economy," said Sumner.

Merit scowled.

That left movies and books and culture.

I didn't expect men to care about hemlines or the latest diet or pin money. But there had to be common ground. "Mel, you care about guns," I observed. "I bet there are plenty of men who'll talk about firearms."

"Only one man in a hundred has anything worthwhile to say on the subject." Her gaze caught on Anarchy. "Your new husband may be one of them."

"Perry knows about guns," said Liz.

"Shotguns?" Mel asked.

Liz's blonde hair bounced as she nodded. "Shotguns and handguns. He never goes anywhere without one."

"He's carrying a gun now? Really?" The man wore khaki shorts and a golf shirt. Where had he hidden a weapon? I tilted my head and stared.

"Not this minute. He left the gun in our cabin. It's a .22 caliber Luger. A collector's piece."

The sense of impending doom that had slithered down my neck when I was shooting returned. With interest. Guns, alcohol, and something dark swimming below the surface of what appeared to be a perfect summer weekend. My heart clenched and I prayed. *I'm happy for the first time in my adult life. Please, don't let anything happen to Anarchy.*

"Ellison, are you okay?" Liz reached across the table and patted my hand.

I pulled myself away from the terrible memory of Anarchy getting shot, then forced a smile. "I'm fine."

"You look pale. I hope you don't mind that Perry brought a handgun."

"Not at all." Guns didn't bother me. Not unless they were pointed at people—especially people I loved. "Must be the heat." I waved the warm, humid air away from my face.

Her wrinkled forehead said she remained unconvinced of my wellness. "May I get you a glass of water?"

"I'll get it." The caterer who'd been introduced as Misty, gave me a kind smile, then fetched me a glass. "How's dinner?"

"Marvelous," said Liz.

Mel nodded her agreement. "Best potato salad I've ever had." She heaped another spoonful onto her plate. "What's for dessert?"

Misty, who was in her twenties and had a figure that suggest she never ate sweets, replied, "Your choice, watermelon, popsicles, or pineapple upside-down cake."

"Graham's favorite." Sumner pursed her lips as if she disapproved of dessert.

Merit, whose plate was empty, waved a single finger. "Excuse me, I don't eat fried food, or anything with dairy, or cane sugar, or wheat. What else do you have?"

Merit was a woman with a great mind. She plumbed the depths. Her understanding of physics and philosophy and philately were profound, but did she ever let loose and have fun? Fun that did not include equations, Kant or a single stamp. Fun that did include delicious fried chicken, laughter with her friends, and pineapple upside-down cake.

"No asking Misty for special orders," Willa declared.

We stared at her. Willa never put her foot down.

"I mean it," she insisted. "Catering for a group this large is hard enough. If you won't eat meat, try the vegetables. Then, have watermelon for dessert."

Merit sniffed but added tomatoes and cucumber slices to her plate.

I took a sip of cool water and caught Anarchy's eye. Was he bored? Annoyed that I'd insisted we come? Enjoying himself?

He waved a chicken leg my way and grinned, and my shoulders relaxed.

"Ellison." Buffy caught my attention. "Are you traveling this summer?"

"We're just back from our honeymoon." We'd spent glorious weeks in Italy. Just the two of us.

"Surely, you're taking Grace on a trip. Have you visited Anarchy's family?"

Take my daughter to see Anarchy's parents? I'd do that right after I pinned paper wings to a pig and taught it to fly.

"I met his mother at your wedding reception. Doesn't she live in San Francisco?"

"Palo Alto. What about you? What are your travel plans for the summer?"

"We're splitting time between Colorado and Michigan."

"Mountains and a big lake?"

"Exactly. Although Bill will travel to and from Kansas City often." She frowned as if she worried that he'd find a girlfriend in her absence. "He'll be home alone. Might I prevail upon you to ask him for dinner a few times?"

I was newly, blissfully married and could have no interest in her husband. "We'd be delighted."

As the sun dipped, and the sky turned to dark velvet, one of Misty's servers pulled out a guitar. The woman was young, early twenties I guessed, and her long hair was parted in the middle of her scalp. She looked like Joni Mitchell but sang a John Denver tune. "Almost heaven..."

Charlie, who'd starred in our high school musicals, joined her. By the chorus, we all sang. Even Merit, and I registered surprise that she knew the words to a popular song.

As the last "country roads" faded into the twilight, the singer grinned at us, then launched into "Love Will Keep Us Together." Perry pulled Liz from her seat at the picnic table, and the two danced.

There were so many fireflies, it seemed as if the night sky twinkled around us. Above us, away from the city lights, the stars were near blinding.

Anarchy's breath brushed against my ear. "Dance?"

"I'd love to." I stood and melted into his strong arms.

Overcome by romance, or gin, everyone quickly abandoned the picnic table.

A few couples faded into the darkness.

Anarchy and I danced. When the young woman finished with Captain and Tennille, she went back to John Denver, and we swayed to "Annie's Song."

Lost in the night's magic, I whispered, "Maybe I was wrong."

Anarchy pulled me closer. "About?"

"This weekend being a disaster."

Again, his breath touched my ear. "From where I'm standing, it looks amazing."

My heart fluttered, and I tilted my head to steal a kiss. My lips parted, and I gazed into Anarchy's perfect coffee-brown eyes. He gazed back. Enchantment sparkled around us. Electricity arced between us, and warm honey replaced the blood in my veins. This—dancing with Anarchy—was perfection.

"Tired?" he asked.

"Not remotely."

His eyes sparkled. "That doesn't mean we shouldn't turn in."

My heart and stomach competed in a fluttering competition. "Sounds like a good—"

A scream pierced the night.

Anarchy pulled me closer and stiffened. His head swiveled, looking for danger, ready to protect me.

A woman streaked past us. Buffy screamed again. "Snake!"

I leapt from Anarchy's arms and flew to the picnic table without actually touching the ground. My boot-clad feet knocked over a mason jar filled with flowers and my heel ground into a dirty plate, but I couldn't bring myself to care.

The singer gaped at me—at us. Buffy was on the table with me.

Anarchy's brow wrinkled with concern. "Ellison?"

"You heard her. Snake." I scanned the ground. Was that long line a shadow or a serpent? The muscles in my back and neck were so tight, my ribs hurt.

My husband blinked at me, and I got the impression he was trying to hide a grin. "You're safe on the table?"

Exactly. Buffy was on the table with me. I clutched her arm. There was strength in numbers. "Liz? Join us?" She had bare ankles. Didn't she realize she was in danger?

She shook her head and grinned. "I only leap on tables for mice."

Poor, foolish Liz. "What do you think the snake was hunting?"

Now she looked nervous.

"What kind of snake?" Anarchy asked Buffy.

I huffed. "Does it matter?" It did not. Snakes were snakes. And snakes were scary. Probably evil.

"It was black," said Buffy. "Like a nightmare."

"Like a rat snake," said Perry.

"Rat?" Liz squeaked "There are rats?"

"No, dear," Perry promised. "No rats."

"You're sure?" She eyed my spot on the table as if she might join me. I held out my hand to help her.

"No rats," Perry repeated. "And the snake is harmless." He gave me a pointed stare. "It won't hurt you."

Ha! A likely story. I would not be talked down. "I don't care if it's a six-inch garter snake. I want assurances it's gone."

"It wasn't six-inches." Buffy spread her arms wide. "It was enormous."

That settled it. I wasn't leaving the table.

"You're wearing boots," Thatch observed.

"They only reach mid-calf." My fear of snakes wasn't reasonable. I *knew* that. But sometimes emotion and reason were very far apart. And when it came to reptiles that slithered and hissed and sank fangs into unsuspecting ankles, there was no room for reason.

"Ellison." Anarchy extended his hand. "I'll protect you."

"Nope. Get rid of the snake, and I'll get down."

"It won't hurt you," said the Joni Mitchell look-alike. "It's probably more scared than you are."

First off, no one asked for her opinion. Second, her assertion was ridiculous. I was nearly frozen in terror.

When Grace was eight, my late husband and I had rented a house at Lake of the Ozarks, and on our first night there, the two of them hid a rubber snake in my bed.

I turned back the covers and screamed so loud the neighbors across the cove were certain I was being brutally murdered. They called the police, and my husband had to explain that he'd merely scared me out of my wits.

I didn't blame Grace. She was a child playing a joke on her mother. I did blame Henry. He'd known my fear, financed the purchase of the damned snake, and laughed at my terror.

At least Anarchy wasn't laughing at me. "I'll carry you to the cabin."

"It's too far."

"Buffy, get down," said Bill.

"Nope." She crossed her arms. Buffy was a smart woman.

"I mean it Buffy. Get down from there."

"No."

Bill stepped closer to the table. "You're embarrassing me." He spoke so low only Buffy and I heard him. "It's a snake, not the boogeyman."

"I'd rather face the boogeyman," Buffy replied.

Amen, sister. In that, we were in complete agreement.

"Now, Buffy."

"No."

"Maybe if we dispatch the snake?" Anarchy suggested.

"It's a rat snake. We want rat snakes. They keep the rodent population in check." Bill was the opposite of helpful.

"I meant we could take it to the woods."

"It will come back," said Buffy. She directed a scalding glare at her husband. "The only good snake is a dead snake."

I wouldn't go that far. I couldn't countenance killing something just because it scared me. But I wasn't getting off the table until it was gone.

"Ellison." Anarchy smiled up at me. "Do you see a snake?"

"No. But it could be lurking in the shadows. It's black, I wouldn't see it."

"If I promise to protect you, will you get down?"

Bill muttered something about molly-coddling, held his hand out to his wife, and said, "Get down, now."

Buffy and I exchanged a look. Only we understood the fear.

"Bill's afraid of being locked in a small space." She glared at him. "He'd do anything to avoid it."

Bill shrugged. "Plenty of people have claustrophobia."

"And plenty of people have ophidiophobia."

I was impressed Buffy knew the scientific term for being scared out of my mind by a scaly, hissing demon.

"I read a third of all adults are scared of snakes," she added. If that were true, there should be more people on the picnic table. In truth, I wasn't only afraid of actual snakes. Just thinking about snakes scared me. Seeing them in movies or television or seeing their pictures in books was equally awful. And the reptile room at the zoo? I skirted that building by at least fifty yards.

"You two are being ridiculous," said Bill

Anarchy stiffened. "Ellison can't help her fear. Neither can your wife."

"They don't have to act like children."

Buffy fisted her hands. "Let's lock you in a jail cell and see how you do."

Bill paled.

"Yeah," called Graham. "How would you like a prison cell, Bill?

Bill's brows drew together, and he bared his teeth. "Stay out of this, Graham."

The lawyer held up his hands in mock surrender. "Just saying, people who live in glass houses—"

"Shouldn't throw stones." Buffy glowered at her husband.

"Ellison," said Anarchy. "I'm sure the snake is gone."

"How?"

"It's been five minutes, and no one has seen it. Also—" he glanced at my feet "—you're wearing boots. Please?"

I hesitated.

"I'll carry you."

That was just silly. I weighed far too much for him to carry me all the way to cabin. Not that the idea didn't hold appeal.

"Fine." I took Anarchy's hand and allowed him to help me down. Then, I apologized to the caterer. "I'm sorry about your tablecloth."

"I get it." Her smile was sweet and seemed genuine. "I don't like snakes either."

"C'mon Buffy," groused Bill. "Get down."

Gingerly, and without her husband's assistance, Buffy descended the table. "It's a good thing you're honest," she told him. "Because, if you ever get arrested, you can rot in a tiny cell. Don't call me for bail."

CHAPTER THREE

*T*here was no coffee. No. Coffee. No grounds. No beans. Nothing.

How had I missed the lack of a coffeemaker in the cabin's tiny kitchen? No sunny yellow gingham face. No sparkling pot. No gurgle of bliss.

How could someone assign me a cabin without the means to brew my morning necessity?

With barely contained annoyance, I jammed my feet into my boots and stepped outside.

The morning, barely dawned, was still cool and the scent of fresh-cut hay perfumed the air, a smell almost as delectable as fresh-brewed coffee.

"Hold on." Anarchy joined me on the cabin's front deck. He wore low-slung pajama bottoms and nothing else. "I want a kiss before you go."

"Coffee." I would not be seduced.

He caught my waist and pulled me close. "You need a reason to hurry back."

"Coffee."

"A kiss first."

It wasn't as if kissing my husband was a chore. When my arms wrapped around his neck, and our lips met. I forgot coffee. And the passage of time. And my name.

We separated, and I sighed.

His lips brushed against my ear. "Ten minutes, Ellison."

"What?"

"Coffee or no coffee, you're back in bed in ten minutes."

Who was I to argue? "Deal." I glanced at my watch and hesitated. Five-fifty. What kind of crazy left their new husband for coffee? But...coffee.

The gravel on the path to the club's main building crunched beneath my soles. Surely at the clubhouse there would be— please, God—fresh-brewed coffee. I paused and glanced over my shoulder.

Anarchy leaned against the cabin's door frame with his arms crossed over his muscled chest. He caught me looking and offered a naughty grin.

Who needed coffee?

I did. And I needed it badly.

Despite Libba's smirking assertion that newlyweds didn't sleep, I required at least six hours of shut-eye each night. The deafening roar of the air-conditioner had ensured I got considerably less than that. Well, the AC and Anarchy.

Coffee.

Only its siren song was strong enough to lure me away from my husband and his sleep-mussed hair and his eyes that glowed with promise.

I hurried my steps. The sooner I got coffee, the sooner I could return to Anarchy, whose bedroom eyes signaled he'd decided to forego fishing for other more pleasurable pursuits.

I pushed open the clubhouse door, spotted a coffee urn, and moaned my appreciation.

"Good morning, Mrs. Jones." Misty offered me a tired smile.

"Good morning." I nodded at the urn. "And bless you."

"I can't function without coffee." Misty was a woman after my own heart.

I shoved a Styrofoam cup under the spigot, and my mouth watered as steaming nectar poured forth. "I'm the same." I added cream to the cup and took my first sip.

In heaven, angels sang.

Misty lifted her own cap in salute, as if she understood the transformative experience.

I took a second sip, and a third, then I was ready to conduct a polite conversation. "Dinner was wonderful."

A soft shade of pink colored her cheeks, and she ducked her head. "Until the snake?"

I suppressed a shudder. "Until the snake."

"You left at the right time."

"Oh?"

"Talk turned to politics."

Ah. President Ford's intention to run for re-election—or actual election—had many in the Republican party on edge. They believed he was painted by Nixon's crooked brush, and his running for office would ensure a win for the Democrats. "Tempers flared?"

Misty's blue eyes clouded, and a crease marred her smooth forehead. "You could say that."

"Tonight will be better." Such wishful thinking. "What are you serving?"

"Barbeque. Maybe the smoke will keep the snakes away."

"One can hope." I took another blissful sip. "Do you do this often? Cater whole weekends, I mean."

"This is the first time."

I refilled my now-empty cup, then reached for a second. "For my husband."

She held up her free hand. "No judging. I've been known to pour a backup mug."

Truly, a woman after my own heart. "I can't start my

morning without it."

She nodded in understanding, then glanced at her watch. "Breakfast service starts at eight."

"What time is it?"

"Just before six."

"What's for breakfast?"

"Scrambled eggs, bacon, and my special cinnamon rolls."

My mouth watered. "Sounds delicious." I moved toward the door. "Thank you for the coffee."

While I was inside, the sky had shifted from pink to lemon yellow. The last traces of the mist laced through the short grass and the smell of a new day, fresh with possibilities, brought a smile to my lips. Yesterday's dread seemed far away. I stepped onto the path.

"Good morning." Sumner ran toward me from farther down the path. She wore running shoes, gym shorts and a sweaty tee-shirt. And fake eyelashes. Who went running in fake eyelashes?

Rather than ask, I said, "You're dedicated." I'd brought paints, not running shoes to this getaway.

"I can't eat like I did last night and not exercise. And it gets too hot to run later in the day." She slowed her pace to a walk and wiped her brow.

"I'm giving myself the weekend off." Come Monday, Max, our Weimaraner, would drag me around Loose Park until I made him stop. And, since life was easier when Max was tired, I'd let him run until he dropped.

Together, we walked toward our cabins. A quick walk. I'd spent most of my ten minutes chatting to Misty. I might have exceeded the allotted time.

Sumner glanced at my full hands. "Two cups?"

"One's for Anarchy." I sounded defensive, as if I expected her to call me out on my addiction.

"I hoped to chat with your husband last night. Hold on—"

she bent, rested her hands on her knees, and stretched her back. "But the snake—"

"I know, I know." Hopping onto the table at a dinner party had not been my finest moment. "I heard things got interesting after we left."

"Gin and politics don't mix." She straightened and glanced again at my full hands. "I thought Anarchy was going fishing with Graham. Haven't they left?"

"I don't know what they worked out, but when I went to get coffee, Graham hadn't knocked on our door." I hoped he hadn't knocked in my absence. I had a fantasy that involved drinking coffee in bed.

Summer frowned. "It's not like Graham to dally. Maybe he drank more than I thought."

"If they've left for the lake, you're welcome to Anarchy's coffee." The offer was reluctant. And generous.

"No, thank you. I'm a tea drinker."

I had nothing against tea. It just wasn't coffee. "This is me." I nodded toward our cabin and slowed my steps.

Sumner walked on. "I'll see you at breakfast."

Breakfast. "Misty is making cinnamon rolls. From scratch."

"Sounds del—" Sumner tripped and fell.

With my hands full of coffee, I couldn't help her. "Are you all right?"

She made no move to get up off the gravel. "I'm not sure."

"Hold on." I set the coffee cups on the cabin's front porch, hurried to Sumner's side, crouched, and grasped her elbow. "Can you stand?"

Her forehead creased. "I think so."

With me lifting, we got her back on her feet. She swayed.

"Where are you hurt?"

"I'm not sure. I feel shaky. My ankle?"

"Come on. Let's get you to your cabin, then I'll get Buffy." Our friend had worked as a nurse before she married.

I supported Sumner to the three steps that led to her cabin's front porch. Rather than lead her up the stairs, I climbed them and knocked on the door.

Graham didn't answer.

"Graham?"

No answer.

I looked back at Sumner, who waited at the bottom of the stairs.

Her lips were a thin line, and she looked pale. "He should be up."

"Graham?" Louder this time.

Sumner swayed, then steadied herself with the short handrail. "Maybe he went fishing."

"You need to sit down." Her ankle might be sprained. She needed elevation and ice. "Graham, I'm coming in." I tried the handle, and the door swung open.

Over the past year, I'd seen terrible things. Clowns with knives. Heads in ovens. Bodies beneath cars. Anarchy shot. But this? I stared. Horrified. Then I squeezed my eyes shut.

"Ellison, what's wrong?"

Graham was dead. A lake of blood surrounded his body, and his eyes stared sightlessly at the ceiling.

"Ellison?"

The woman waiting at the bottom of the stairs deserved an answer. "Um…"

She stared at me as if I were a few cards short of a full deck. "What's wrong?"

"We need Anarchy."

"Why?"

Because he was a homicide detective with actual practice telling family members their loved ones were dead. "It looks as if Graham…had an accident." Lie. Graham didn't accidentally create that red bloom on the left side of his chest. But what else could I say?

"Is Graham okay?"

The opposite of okay. "Let me get Anarchy." I rushed down the steps, ran to our cabin, and threw open the door. "I need you."

"Likewise." He studied my face, and his sexy smile faltered. "What's wrong?"

"Next cabin over. It's Graham." I lowered my voice. "He's dead."

"Sumner?"

"Just back from a run. She's waiting outside."

He nodded. Once. Then he pulled on a shirt and strode past me.

I joined Sumner at the bottom of the stairs and watched my husband disappear into her cabin.

"What happened?" she demanded.

"Did you or Graham bring a gun this weekend?"

She was already pale, but the remaining color drained from her face. "Graham brought a shotgun."

I hadn't looked too closely at Graham's bloody chest. Had a shotgun caused the damage?

"Ellison, is Graham all right?"

"It looks as if he's been shot."

She snorted. "Don't be ridiculous."

I had no answer to that. What had happened to Sumner's husband was the opposite of ridiculous. It was horrid and terrifying and evil. My throat thickened, and tears wet my eyes.

She studied my face. "You're not joking."

"No."

She hauled herself up the stairs. "Graham!"

Anarchy stopped her at the cabin's entrance.

"No. Let me by. What happened to Graham? Graham!"

"I'm sorry—"

She shoved at his chest. "Let me in! Graham!"

Anarchy shifted to the left and let Sumner see her husband's body.

"That can't be. I've only been gone for less than an hour." Again she pushed against Anarchy. "I need to see him."

He didn't budge. "It's a crime scene."

She peered around the arm blocking her way, and her shoulders crumpled. Then her knees. Then she sank onto the wooden deck. "Ellison said it was an accident. It has to be an accident. No one would hurt Graham."

She wasn't thinking clearly. Anyone with a functioning brain would notice there was no gun near Graham's body. Whoever shot him had taken the weapon with them. Also, in hindsight, I shouldn't have lied. Graham Landingham's death was no accident.

"Ellison." Anarchy claimed my attention. "I need to call this in."

There were no phones in the cabins. "How?"

He closed the door on Graham's murder. "The main clubhouse. Can you stay here? Keep the scene secure?" His troubled gaze landed on Sumner, then he caught my gaze. *Could I take care of Sumner?*

"Yes." To all his questions. This was not my first body. I knelt next to my friend.

Her shoulders slumped. Her head hung. And her back shuddered as if she fought racking sobs.

Anarchy offered me an approving nod, then strode toward the main building.

I rubbed a gentle circle on Sumner's back.

"It can't be true," she moaned.

It was. But that wasn't exactly comforting. I searched for something to say. I should have some idea. After all, I'd found my first husband's body. Hoping for inspiration, I breathed deep. The sweetness of the morning had soured, tainted by blood and death and the impending investigation. "I'm so sorry for your loss."

"Who would do this? Everyone loved Graham."

"They did." It was a good thing I wasn't Pinocchio. My nose would have grown by two feet just this morning.

At eight o'clock, the guests gathered in the dining room at the clubhouse.

Anarchy and a cluster of deputies gathered near the coffee urn. The rest of us poked at eggs and barely tasted Misty's cinnamon rolls.

I sipped coffee and wished I was still in Italy.

"What happened, Ellison?" asked Charlie. His usually clear eyes were rimmed with red and his cheeks were the color of old fish.

I shared a table for four with Charlie, Libba, and Buffy. "I don't know."

"Your cabin is next to theirs." Libba looked almost as rough as her boyfriend. She'd added blush to her cheeks and mascara to her tired eyes. "Surely you heard something."

"Not over that air conditioner."

"Bill saw Sumner running around five-thirty." Compared to Libba and Charlie, Buffy looked positively bright eyed.

And she'd told me something Anarchy would want to know. I made a mental note to share.

"He saw her on his way up here to fill his thermos with coffee. They said hello, then he went fishing."

It was just after six when I'd found Graham's body. That gave the killer approximately thirty minutes. "Did Bill come back to the cabin after he got coffee?"

"He went fishing. The police pulled him off the water. He

told me then." She frowned. "I can't believe you and your detective husband missed the sound of a gunshot."

"You know the roar of the crowd when the Chiefs score a touchdown?"

She nodded.

"Our air conditioner is louder. Someone could wander cabin to cabin with a howitzer, and we'd miss the whole thing."

She leaned forward. "Who does your husband suspect?"

Libba and Charlie lifted their heavy heads and joined Buffy in staring at me.

"I don't know that he suspects anyone."

Buffy pursed her lips. "The police asked us not to leave."

Libba shrugged, then winced as if the slightest movement made her headache worse. "We're staying through tomorrow anyway."

"That was before Graham got murdered." Buffy made a fair point.

"We were his friends. We should do what we can to ensure the killer is caught." Lord, that sounded sanctimonious. I offered up an apologetic half-smile.

"Are they sure it wasn't suicide?" Did Buffy know something, did Graham have a reason to kill himself? What were Graham's secrets?

"It wasn't suicide."

"How do you know?" she insisted.

"I saw the body." Found the body.

Anarchy broke away from the cluster of police and approached our table. "Ellison, a word?"

"Of course." I stood and followed him outside.

The sun was up. The sky was blue. The birds were singing. And I wanted to crawl into bed and pull the covers over my head.

"You okay?" he asked.

"Fine."

He rubbed the back of his neck. "The sheriff's department isn't equipped to investigate a murder."

"What does that mean?"

"KCPD loaned me to their department."

A lead weight settled in my stomach. "You're investigating? He gave a brief nod.

"Our friends. You're investigating our friends."

"One of them is a killer."

"The rest are not." I knew how this went. Secrets spilled in murder investigations. Ugly, life-changing secrets. And those secrets didn't necessarily belong to the killer.

"Graham deserves justice."

"No argument. But can't someone else find the murderer?" Perhaps it was selfish, but I didn't want my husband investigating our friends. They might—and that was an enormous might—forgive him for doing his job, but they wouldn't forget that he was the one who discovered an affair, a hidden bank account, or a predilection worth killing for.

"I'm here. I know the suspects. Both my police chief and the county sheriff think I'm the man for the job."

"You know the suspects?" My voice was too high. I took a deep breath and tried again. "You more than know the suspects. They're our friends."

"They're your friends." His words were as sharp as a slap on the cheek. "And one of them killed Landingham."

"Maybe someone snuck onto the property." It was unlikely, but I'd clutch at any straw.

"Ellison."

"It could happen."

"We'll investigate that, too. But it's more likely someone already here killed him."

"The staff?"

"The staff he met for the first time yesterday?"

"You don't know that. Maybe he knew one of them before.

Misty catered for his law firm. He could have met her servers at an event."

"We'll look into that."

I stared at my boots. The toes were scuffed, and dust had settled into the stitching.

"Ellison."

"Give me a minute." I wanted so badly for Anarchy to fit into my life that I'd never given a thought as to how I'd fit into his. He was a cop. A homicide detective. He asked questions. Solved murders. I knew that. But this? Who knew what secrets he'd expose? I scraped my fingers through my hair.

"Graham deserves justice."

"I know. You already said that."

"What's your concern? Invitations to cocktail parties?"

I jerked my head so I could glare at him. Did he think so little of me? I wanted my friends to like him. I wanted Anarchy to like them. I wanted them to be *our* friends. Part of the life we built together. "This has nothing to do with parties." It had everything to do with us. "Judges recuse themselves."

"Pardon?"

"When they have a personal interest in a case." I was on to something. "They recuse themselves. Another judge takes over. You could do that."

"I could. But it will affect my career."

The lead in my stomach reached up and squeezed my heart.

His hands closed around my shoulders. "I'm sorry."

That utterly stupid line from *Love Story* landed on the tip of my tongue. *Love means never having to say you're sorry.* Real love meant saying *you're right, I'm wrong, I'm sorry.* But who was wrong? Me? Anarchy?

He loved his job, and I knew what he did when I married him. Was it fair of me to ask him not to investigate a murder just because I worried our friends wouldn't like him? "Do what you have to do."

"I can walk away."

I searched the face I loved so well. Anarchy's brows were drawn, his eyes serious, and his lips tight. He'd damage his career. For me. "You don't want to walk away."

"No," he admitted.

"Then catch Graham's killer."

CHAPTER FOUR

The police—Anarchy and a wet-behind-the-ears deputy from the county sheriff's office—chose the clubhouse dining room to conduct interviews.

With a brief nod, Anarchy told me I could leave. I escaped to the stables, where the comforting smells of horses and leather filled my lungs. Usually when I was upset, I painted. The transfer of color from palette to canvas helped me work through emotions. But painting was a solitary pursuit, and Libba and Charlie had followed me.

I'd let them. I didn't want to be alone.

Unwilling to risk her manicure, Libba leaned against a stall and watched as Charlie and I prepared the horses.

"Anarchy let you leave?" It was rhetorical question. I dragged the hoof pick through a bit of manure caught near the horse's shoe.

"He didn't want you to be alone."

I grunted, satisfied there were no pebbles or small rocks caught in Nester's hoof, and let him stand on four legs.

"Are you okay?" she asked.

"Fine."

"You don't look fine."

Not compared to Libba. She'd taken a moment to go back to her cabin and change.

"Jods? Who wears jodhpurs to go on a trail ride?" Or makeup?

"They look good on me." She twisted her hips and preened.

Charlie grinned his appreciation.

"Whatever."

She scrunched her nose at me. "You're in a mood."

"I found a body."

"Pish." She studied her nails. They were painted a vibrant crimson and matched her lipstick. "You find bodies all the time."

"Anarchy's investigating."

"That happens all the time, too."

"Not like this. He'll ask everyone here uncomfortable questions." I threw a blanket and saddle on Nester's back, then adjusted the horse's girth and patted his neck. I'd ridden the gelding before and knew he puffed his stomach during saddling. When he finally exhaled, the girth would be loose. "Stop holding your breath, Nester."

"So what's new about Anarchy asking questions?" Libba had been on the receiving end of Anarchy's uncomfortable questions. More than once.

The questions seemed more intrusive now that he was my husband. "I want him to feel as if he's a part of my life."

She frowned. "He does. The man adores you." Libba tilted her head and her frown cleared as a light dawned. "You're worried that he'll offend someone, that the kids on the playground will be mean to him."

I scowled at her, then slipped my fingers under the girth. Still tight.

"You are!" She grinned at her ability to bulldoze through my psyche. "Anarchy doesn't care about being included in the right foursome for golf." She tapped her lips with a red nail. "Does Anarchy even play golf?"

"No." The admission cost me.

"The man cares about you, Grace, and his job. Period."

Charlie led a bay mare to the stall where Libba oversaw our efforts. "Do you need a leg up?"

"I've got it." Libba hefted herself into the saddle, then adjusted the reins. "And justice. Anarchy also cares about justice."

Rather than answer, I gave Nester's girth a final check. Loose. I tightened it, jammed my left foot in the stirrup, and swung my right leg over the horse's broad back.

Charlie mounted his gelding, and the three of us rode out into the morning sun.

I blinked as my eyes adjusted to the brightness. "Shall we head for the woods?"

"Graham was a monumental ass," said Libba. "But even he deserves justice. That's Anarchy's job."

She wasn't going to let this go. I searched for a topic that might divert her from her Anarchy-is-right-and-Ellison-is-being-ridiculous rut. "I thought you liked Graham."

She and Charlie exchanged a loaded glance.

"What?"

Charlie cleared his throat.

"What?" I repeated.

Charlie held the reins in his left hand and rubbed the back of his neck with his right. "I might have threatened him."

Oh dear Lord. "Why?"

"Graham was digging into my past."

"Why?" Getting a substantive answer out of Charlie was like pulling teeth. Also, what deep, dark secret could he have?

"Graham had an investigator talk to my ex-wife. She's not my biggest fan, and she's looking for a reason to deny visitation rights."

"Why would Graham do that?"

"There's a doctor in my department who expected to get my job. He's trying to prove he's the more qualified candidate, and that I got the job through nepotism." Charlie had moved back to Kansas City to run a department at St. Mark's Hospital. "It's ridiculous. But Adams hired Graham. If he wins, I could lose my job. Maybe my kids."

"When did you threaten him?"

"Last night." Charlie shifted in his saddle. "But it was just a threat. I'm in the business of saving lives, not taking them."

"What happened?"

"Graham told Charlie the lawsuit and investigation weren't personal," said Libba. "He said Charlie needed to lighten up."

We'd reached the trees and riding abreast wasn't possible on the narrow path through the woods. We slipped into a line. Charlie went first, then me, then Libba.

"The lawsuit and investigation feel damn personal to me." Charlie twisted in his saddle and gave me—no, Libba—a look. "I wouldn't have come if I knew the Landinghams would be here."

"I didn't know." She sounded aggrieved, as if she'd heard that complaint already.

"Who exactly put this weekend together?" I asked.

"Liz and Willa," Libba replied. "I never dreamed they'd invite Graham and Sumner. Graham was trying to oust Thatch as managing partner and he stole Perry's biggest client. Why would they include them?"

It didn't make sense. Not unless…Nope. My mind wasn't going there.

"Charlie, what did you say to Graham?"

"I told him what I thought of him," he replied.

"Graham replied that if he hadn't taken the case, another lawyer would have," said Libba.

I had yet to hear a threat. "And?"

"I told him he'd get what was coming to him."

"That's it?"

"I did not tell him I'd knife him in the back. Which is what he did to me. I've known the man my whole life, and he betrayed me for a quick buck." Charlie's horse tossed its head.

"Ease up on the reins," Libba advised.

Charlie ducked his chin and loosened his hold on his mount's mouth.

Dappled sunlight pebbled our path. My saddle creaked. Charlie's horse whinnied. The morning seemed almost perfect —except for the dead lawyer and the man ahead of me, who'd threatened said lawyer. The night before the murder.

"How long has it been since you've ridden trails?" asked Libba.

"Too long. Don't change the subject."

"There's nothing to talk about, Ellison. Charlie got mad at Graham. He said something foolish, but he didn't mean it—"

"Oh, I meant it. But I didn't act on it."

"As you wish. He meant it, but he didn't kill Graham. He wouldn't. There's nothing left to discuss." Nearly four decades of friendship meant I heard the doubt hiding in Libba's tone. Did Charlie hear the same thing?

I let Charlie's guilt or innocence go. For now. "Misty said tempers were running high all around."

Libba snorted. "Let's just say Merit and Graham didn't agree on the direction of the country. President Ford deciding to run for a second term is causing some angst."

"At least she got to discuss ideas." And prove she had a great mind.

Libba barked a short laugh. "I'm not sure she enjoyed it. She left in tears."

"Why?" That didn't sound like Merit.

"Graham called her a patronizing twit."

"That's not so bad." It wasn't polite, but he could have called her an uptight bitch.

"He also told her she had a stick up her keister."

"Ah." That covered the uptight part.

"She looked at Tommy for support, but he shrugged as if he agreed."

"Yikes." Not the response a woman hoped for from her husband.

"Then she called Graham a money-grubbing bottom-feeder."

"And?"

"He told her he wasn't the only money-grubber at the table. When Tommy remained quiet, she asked if he was going to allow that kind of talk."

"And?"

"He told her if she insisted on picking fights, she should learn how to win them."

"Wow." Not wrong, but wow.

"No kidding. She burst into tears and ran off into the night."

"And then?"

"Then there was an awkward silence."

I bet. "What did Tommy say?"

Charlie chuckled. "He talked about John Mayberry's stats."

"Who is John Mayberry?"

"He plays first base for the Royals."

"That's it? Baseball stats?"

"He drank," Charlie added. "A lot. We all did."

For a half-second, I was grateful for the snake that caused my early departure. "Which client?"

"What are you talking about?" asked Libba.

"You said Graham stole Perry's biggest client." I turned in my saddle and looked at her. "Which one?"

"How would I know?" She pursed her lips and tilted her head. "I did hear it was worth millions to the firm." Scrunched her face. "A tobacco company?"

"I asked you earlier who Perry would support for managing

partner, and you told me to ask Liz." She could have told me that Perry had a beef with Graham.

"Things have changed."

Because Graham was dead. Thatch didn't have to worry about competition for his managing partner's job. "What happens now? With the client, I mean."

"I assume Perry will resume his role as lead counsel."

Inwardly, I groaned. In thirty minutes, I'd found three people with reasons to kill Graham. Four if you counted Liz, who would do anything for Perry. And I had a feeling the number of suspects would multiply.

Hopefully, Anarchy had found a gun marked by bloody fingerprints or a witness who'd noticed the killer sneaking to or from Graham's cabin. Hopefully, my friends would be cleared of suspicion.

I wasn't that lucky.

One horse ride, one shower, and one much-need nip of brandy (thank you, Libba) later, and my feet dragged me toward the main clubhouse.

"Mrs. Jones?" Misty appeared on the path. Despite her eyes being red and puffy, the young woman was still pretty. She gave me a tremulous smile.

"Are you all right?" I asked.

She nodded. "Yes. I—you. You found Mr. Landingham?"

"I did."

"It's so awful."

Murder was bone-chilling and reprehensible and awful. Most people went their whole lives without having to really consider the taking of a human life. Sure, they might read an Agatha Christie and treat death as a puzzle, but when the victim was someone they knew, the mystery was overwhelmed by the horror. I was willing to bet a trip to Italy that this was Misty's first brush with violent death. "Terrible," I agreed.

She kicked at a stick on the path. "I have so much I should be doing. Lunch isn't going to serve itself. But I can't focus. Does your husband know who killed Graham?"

"I haven't seen my husband since breakfast, so I don't have an answer to that. Unless there was a witness, I doubt he has the case solved."

"He asked me questions."

"Oh?"

She nodded and wiped her eyes. "Who came in for coffee? What time? That sort of thing."

"What did you tell him?"

"Mr. Geller came in first. He filled a thermos. Then you."

I'd filled two cups. "No one else?"

"Maybe. I thought I heard someone, but I was in the kitchen making cinnamon rolls. When I went to the dining room, there was no one there."

"When was that?"

"After Mr. Geller, but before you." She sniffled, then smoothed her hair, caught in a long blonde ponytail. "What will happen?"

"Anarchy will question everyone once. Maybe twice. Then he'll corroborate alibis."

She wrung her hands. "Being questioned was scary. And I don't have an alibi."

"I don't know about that. Bill saw you, then I did. Also, you don't have a motive."

She sniffled, then looked at me as if I'd offered her a longed-for present.

"There were plenty of people with reason to kill Graham." I kept my voice gentle. "I don't think you need to worry."

She wiped the smudged mascara beneath her eyes. "He seemed like such a nice man."

"You didn't know him well."

"He was always kind to me."

"You're young and pretty. Of course he was nice to you."

Her cheeks colored.

"I'm sorry. That wasn't kind." I sounded bitter and old and entirely too jaded by life. "Graham made unpopular decisions."

"Isn't that what leaders do?"

"He wasn't a leader. He was a lawyer. And some of those decisions hurt people who thought he was their friend." I thought of Charlie, then Perry.

"He didn't deserve this."

"No one deserves this." We walked on, and I asked, "Are you headed back to the clubhouse?"

"I am. Like I said, lunch won't fix itself."

We continued our slow walk, as if there were a thousand places we'd rather be than our destination.

"How did you get into catering?"

"I've always loved to cook. Enough so that I found a way to make a living. I struggled at first, but I landed some corporate accounts, and they've made all the difference."

"Like Graham's firm."

"Exactly. I started by catering a few small parties for them, and some of their clients asked for my name. The business has grown organically."

"It sounds like lots of hard work."

"Worth it." She smoothed the front of her t-shirt and glanced briefly at the Misty Eats logo above her left breast. "The firm is still one of my biggest clients. We cater lunches almost every day and cocktail parties several times a month. One of the lawyers had me cater his daughter's wedding."

"You must spend a lot of time there."

"At first I did my own deliveries. As the business has grown, I've added staff."

"And that's how you got to know Graham?"

She nodded. "Yes."

"There you are!" Willa stood near the door to the clubhouse with her hands planted firmly on her linen clad hips. She sounded annoyed, but I couldn't tell if her ire was directed at me, the wife of the man investigating a murder, or Misty, the caterer who was late serving lunch.

I waved.

Willa glanced at her watch and pinched her lips into a tight line. And I had my answer.

Misty hurried her pace, leaving me behind. "I'm sorry Mrs. Cooke, I just needed a few minutes to myself."

"Everyone is hungry."

Not everyone. The thought of food made me feel vaguely nauseated.

"It won't take long to serve. Give me fifteen minutes." Misty slipped past Willa and disappeared into the clubhouse.

Willa tsked. "She's usually so reliable."

"She's upset about the murder."

She ceded my point with a tiny nod. "We're all upset. But she's being paid. Generously."

I didn't argue. "How's Sumner?"

"Buffy gave her a sedative. She's resting in the Geller's cabin."

When I'd counted suspects—Charlie, Merit, Perry, Liz—I'd forgotten Willa's husband. Graham had wanted Thatch's job as managing partner. "So terrible."

Willa nodded. "Awful. To think, someone snuck onto the property and did this."

I was the queen of wishful thinking, but not even I believed a random person wandered into Graham's cabin and shot him. "You think a stranger did this?"

"The alternative is too terrible to contemplate." She stared down her patrician nose. "Although your husband has no problem making us all seem guilty."

Apparently, Anarchy had asked her uncomfortable questions. What did Willa have to hide? "He's just doing his job."

"Ellison, we're your friends, not suspects."

Right now, they were both. "Anarchy will clear everyone as soon as possible." I crossed my fingers behind my back.

"By asking where we slept? And with whom?" She sounded scandalized.

"Thatch is your alibi, and you are his."

"I shouldn't need an alibi."

But Thatch did? "That's one of the inconvenient things about a murder investigation. Everyone needs to account for their whereabouts."

She sniffed her displeasure. "I notice you didn't hang around for questioning this morning. You disappeared."

"I went riding."

"The perks of being a detective's wife." Her tone was almost snide.

"The perks of having an airtight alibi."

She raised her brows.

"I was with Anarchy until five-fifty. I walked directly to the clubhouse, where I talked to Misty. When I left, I was with Sumner. I didn't have time to kill Graham. Or motive." Unlike her husband.

We stared at each other. Her expression was chilly. Mine was stubborn.

Willa looked away first. "I'm sorry. This whole thing has been so upsetting. I know you had nothing to do with Graham's death. And I know you're not responsible for your husband's questions."

"Graham was murdered." I had doubts and reservations about Anarchy questioning our friends, but I'd never, ever let anyone outside my closest circle know that. To the world, I stood by my man. "If it weren't Anarchy asking those questions, it would be the county sheriff."

Willa huffed as if the whole situation was designed to ruin her weekend.

"I have a question for you."

She checked her watch. "I should check on Misty."

"It's a quick one."

"Well, what is it?"

"You and Liz put this weekend together?"

"That's your question?"

"There's a follow-up."

She lifted a single brow.

"Why did you include Sumner and Graham?"

She stiffened, and her willowy posture looked suddenly brittle. "What do you mean?"

"Wasn't Graham attempting to take over as managing partner?"

She waved at the air as if she'd sensed an annoying mosquito. "Yes. But Graham and Thatch were colleagues. Friends. Thatch would never put office politics over friendship."

I'd been at the shooting range with Thatch and Graham. I'd observed them. Whatever relationship the two men had had, they weren't friends. I smiled at the woman willing to lie for her husband. "Of course not."

Then, reluctantly, I added Willa to my list of possible suspects.

With a tight smile, she turned on her heel and left me.

I lingered on the path.

Did every single person at the Fin and Feather have a reason to want Graham dead? It sure seemed that way. And with so many motives, how would Anarchy catch the killer?

CHAPTER FIVE

*A*narchy and I skipped lunch. He wasn't hungry (one of Misty's staff spent the morning slipping him cinnamon rolls). And I couldn't eat. Not with the memory of Graham in a pool of blood. Not with wondering who among our friends had killed him.

Instead of tucking into chicken-salad sandwiches, home-made potato chips and fresh cut watermelon, we went in search of Tommy Dodson, the one person who'd failed to show up for Anarchy's questions. Merit claimed he was under the weather. Anarchy didn't consider a headache a good enough reason to duck out of assisting a murder investigation.

So, here we stood on the cabin's front porch. "Tommy?" I used a this-is-a-social-call voice and knocked on the door.

No one responded.

I shot Anarchy a concerned glance and knocked harder. "Tommy, it's Ellison."

Still no response.

"This isn't like him." The day had heated like a—well, like a day in July, and perspiration trickled down my back and my feet sweat in my cowboy boots. I tightened my fist, ready to bang on the darned door until Tommy welcomed us into the air-conditioning.

Anarchy reached past me and turned the handle.

"Oh. That was easy."

Together, we stepped into the cabin. The curtains were drawn, and the tiny room was dark and stuffy. There were clothes strewn over the chairs, dirty glasses in the sink, and an open suitcase on the floor. The place stank of sour sweat and gin, and I wrinkled my nose. "Tommy?"

The man on the bunk bed didn't move.

The single bunk bed.

Merit and Tommy hadn't slept in the same bed.

Suddenly the loud air-conditioner in our cabin didn't seem so awful, not if it meant going to sleep and waking up in Anarchy's arms.

"Dodson." Anarchy's voice held a no-nonsense edge.

"Is he dead?" Because finding two bodies in one day—well, if Mother ever found out, I'd never hear the end of it. Also, I'd be genuinely sad. I liked Tommy. Everyone did. They liked him well enough to tolerate Merit. And it took a lot to tolerate Merit.

Anarchy felt for a pulse. "Not dead."

Thank heavens.

As if to prove Anarchy's point, Tommy groaned.

"What's wrong with him?" Had he been poisoned?

"According to everyone, he drank himself stupid."

"Libba and Charlie said he had a few. But this?" There had to be a problem, because adults didn't drink themselves into oblivion unless they were facing difficulties.

Tommy passed gas, loudly, and the smell in the cabin grew exponentially worse.

"Ugh." I propped open the front door and waved the cool air outside. "Do you think he'll be okay?"

"I do."

"Then, we should go." Tommy was neither dead nor capable of carrying on a conversation. Also, the room stank to high heaven.

Tommy groaned a second time and leaned his head over the side of the bed.

On occasion, Henry had drunk to excess. I knew what came next. "Anarchy, you might want to—"

My warning came too late. Tommy threw up on Anarchy's Chuck Taylors.

And my big, strong, fearless husband squealed like a five-year-old girl.

I grabbed his elbow and pulled him away from the mess. There was a decent chance Tommy might vomit again.

Every other man here wore loafers or boat shoes with their shorts. Not Anarchy. I wondered, briefly, how Anarchy felt about conducting an investigation while wearing khaki shorts, a golf shirt, and sneakers. They were a far-cry from his usual dark pants and plaid jacket. At least the canvas shoes would be easy to rinse. Anarchy pointed at his sneakers, and his mouth opened and shut without forming actual words.

My husband, who could face down a gun-wielding killer, break a hardened criminal in an interrogation room, and generally acted like a superhero, was rendered mute by puke.

"I know." I gave his arm a comforting squeeze. "It's gross. I also know Tommy won't be answering any questions right now. Let's get you cleaned up."

"He threw up on me."

"It happens." Ask any mother. We survived spit-up, stomach flu, and teenagers who discovered the liquor cabinet. We washed countless towels and sheets and scrubbed more commodes than we could shake a toilet brush at.

"Not to me."

"There's a first time for everything." I tugged on him, and we stepped into the sunlight.

Anarchy looked down at his shoes (the bright light wasn't doing them any favors) and his skin took on a worrisome greenish pallor.

Oh, dear Lord. "Don't."

He frowned at me. "Don't what?"

"Sympathy vomit."

"That happens?" He looked horrified. And green.

"Kick off your shoes," I instructed.

"And then what?"

"I'll wash them off."

"They'll be wet."

"You can wear a different pair. Do it."

He kicked off the sneakers, and I moved them a good twenty feet away from him. "Wait here." I hurried back to our cabin, grabbed Anarchy's boots and a clean pair of socks, then returned to my husband. "Put these on."

He complied. "Now what?"

"We go to the barn."

"Why?"

"Wash stall," I explained.

He stared at me for long seconds. "You're very resourceful."

He was just now figuring that out? "You're very squeamish." I picked up his sneakers and held them far from my body, and we walked toward the barn. The poor man still looked a bit green, as if he might lose those cinnamon rolls at any moment. We needed a distraction. "What did you learn this morning?"

"Except for Bill Geller and Sumner, everyone was asleep with their spouses when Graham was killed." His tone told me he'd detected multiple lies.

"In the condition he's in, I doubt Tommy would have missed Merit."

"Good point. But why would she shoot Graham?"

"They had a disagreement after we turned in." Turned in

sounded so much better than ran from a black snake. "Libba says insults were hurled. Merit left in tears."

"Merit left, but not Tommy?"

"Not Tommy. He stayed and drank." Apparently nearly enough to kill himself.

Anarchy rubbed his chin. "She seems mousy. Do you think she has what it takes to shoot a man?"

Mousy? I found Merit to be self-righteous and judgmental, not mousy. "Looks can be deceiving." We stepped into the barn, and I went immediately to the wash stall, placed Anarchy shoes on the concrete near the drain in the floor, and turned on the hose. "Stand back."

Anarchy complied, and I directed a steady stream of water onto his soiled sneakers.

He watched me. "It seems as if you've done this before."

"Cleaned things in a wash stall? Absolutely." Not vomit covered sneakers, but muddy boots, a dog, countless horses, and on one memorable occasion, the stall itself. I'd even walked into the barn and found a goat carcass hanging above the drain. When I finished shrieking, I discovered the men who worked there were preparing for a feast. But horses didn't like the smell of blood. I'd washed the heck out of that stall when the goat was gone.

The sneakers were clean and sopping wet, and I picked them up by the heels. "We can leave them to dry in the sun."

"I doubt I'll wear them again." He stepped close to me—so close, my heart gave an anticipatory flutter. "But thank you for coming to my rescue."

My lips tingled with the urge to kiss him. "My pleasure." Anarchy usually came to my rescue. It was nice to reverse our roles.

He took the shoes from my hands, dropped them into the sawdust beneath our feet, and pulled me still closer. "I'll buy new ones."

Remembering the green hue of cheeks, I didn't argue. If he didn't want to wear shoes that had been covered in another man's vomit, that was his prerogative. "Are you feeling better?"

"I am." His fingers traced the length of my jaw.

"That feels nice."

He paused. "We're in a barn."

"Alone in a barn." Alone except for Nester and the other horses, all of whom had their heads out of their stalls. They watched us with interest.

Anarchy chuckled. "I feel as if we have an audience."

"I guess we do." I pulled back so I could look into his eyes. "This is your chance for a real roll in the hay."

"I always knew you were a country girl at heart."

"Very funny." Clean air and seeing a million stars at night were nice, but I didn't like bugs or dust or snakes. Plus, I needed access to good restaurants, good shopping, and my citified friends.

He stroked my jawline again, and part of my brain melted. Where was the ladder to the hayloft?

"We shouldn't." His voice was a whisper against my ear.

"The horses won't care."

"There's a murder to solve."

"You're a tease."

His chuckle was low and rumbly and did things to my blood. Slow fire things. "I'll make good on my promise later."

Hot fire things.

I swallowed my frustration. At least his arms were still wrapped around me. I could wait until we reached the privacy of our cabin. I forced myself to focus on the murder. "Did everyone give you an alibi? Even Misty?" Crying over a man she hardly knew had struck me as mildly suspicious.

"Misty was in the kitchen all morning. Those cinnamon rolls didn't make themselves. Also, both you and Bill saw her.

"True. What about motives?"

He gave me a tired grin. "I hope you can help me with that. Everyone claimed to like him."

My brow creased. "Come again?"

"People don't like to speak ill of the dead."

"Yes, they do. They just qualify it with a 'bless his heart,' or 'I hate to speak ill of the dead, but...'"

"Well, no one spoke ill to a homicide detective. Graham was a great guy. A great husband. A great lawyer. A great friend. He'll be sorely missed. His passing is a huge loss to the firm, to the community, to his wife."

"I heard six solid motives just this morning."

"Maybe we should put you on the payroll."

"The payroll?" I smiled at him. I tried to smolder. "I could take my salary in kisses."

There was that chuckle again. "Has anyone told you that you're hard to resist?"

"Not recently." I tilted my head, and our lips were but a breath apart.

"A salary paid in kisses? A bargain at twice the price." His lips explored mine.

My body melted, my toes curled, and someone—definitely not a horse—coughed.

Anarchy and I jumped apart as if someone had turned the hose on us.

Liz, who wore a linen peasant dress and looked like she'd walked off the pages of *Town & Country*, and Perry, who wore madras shorts and loafers without socks, stared at us, their cheeks pink with embarrassment.

Perry broke a cheeky grin. "Sorry to interrupt."

Liz stared at the sawdust in the aisle as if she hoped a hole would open and swallow her.

"We wanted to tell you right away," said Liz. Her forehead wrinkled and a furrow cut into the space between her eyes.

"Tell us what?" I asked.

Liz and Perry exchanged a glance, and Perry's grin faltered.

Anarchy, who could use silence as an interrogation technique, said nothing.

"It's gone," Liz blurted.

"What's gone?" Silence was hard for me.

She ran flattened palms over her hair. "Perry's handgun. It's gone. Someone took it."

We had a dead man and a missing gun. And two plus two often made four. "Oh, Lizzie."

"When did you realize it was missing?" asked Anarchy.

"Just now," Liz replied. "We didn't think to check on it before we went to the clubhouse this morning. Then you kept us there." Her annoyance was obvious.

Perry held up a placating hand. "Where we were happy to assist you with your investigation."

"Then we stayed and ate lunch." Liz rubbed her fingers down the sides of her nose. "It was only a few minutes ago we realized it was gone. We came and found you straight away.

"When did you last see the gun?" asked Anarchy.

"Last night," Perry replied. "Before dinner. There's no gun safe, so I put it on the shelf in the closet."

"You didn't check it when you got back to the cabin?"

"I did not," Perry replied. "Everyone had a few drinks. When we got back to the cabin, we were tired. We brushed our teeth, drank a few glasses of water, and went to bed. I never thought to check on the gun."

"This morning?"

"We didn't know *why* we were being called to the clubhouse," Liz explained. "If we knew someone had been shot, we'd have looked. "

Anarchy's face was a cool mask. "You didn't mention the gun when we spoke."

"We thought you knew about it."

"Oh?"

"I told Ellison that Perry brought a handgun when we were at dinner."

I nodded my confirmation. I hadn't thought to tell him because I'd assumed every man here had a handgun. Mel might have two.

"You only told Ellison?"

"Everyone at our end of the table heard me mention it. Probably the service staff, too. Maybe the men sitting closest to us."

I closed my eyes and pictured the table. The men closest had been Fred and Thatch.

Anarchy's voice had me opening my eyes. "Perry, did you tell anyone you'd brought a handgun?"

"I don't recall." Spoken like a lawyer.

"What kind is it?"

"A .22 caliber Luger."

"What time did you leave the party last night?"

The two exchanged a look.

"Not sure," said Liz.

"Who was still at the party?"

"Sumner and Graham, Tommy, Thatch and Willa, and Libba and Charlie."

"Did you lock your cabin when you went to dinner?"

"No."

"So, anyone could have snuck in and taken the gun after you left for dinner?"

Perry offered a rueful nod. "Do you know what killed Graham? Was he shot with a. 22?"

"We don't have ballistics yet."

"But it was a handgun? "

"It appears to be. Remind me of your relationship with Graham."

"We practiced law together."

I waited, hoping Perry would mention the tobacco client.

"For how long?" Anarchy asked.

"How many years does this make, Liz? Sixteen or seventeen?"

"Sixteen."

"There you have it. We've practiced law together for sixteen years."

"Graham was well liked?"

"Lawyers are never well liked. How many lawyers does it take to screw in a light bulb?" He waited a beat. "Three. One to do it, and two sue him for malpractice."

Liz frowned at him. "That joke's not funny, honey lamb."

"Uh-oh. I've been honey lambed." He offered his wife a quick grin. "You'll like this one, Ellison. Why did God make snakes before lawyers?"

I shook my head.

"To practice. Why don't sharks attack lawyers?"

"Perry." Liz's voice was a warning.

A warning he ignored. "Professional courtesy. One More. What did the attorney name his daughter?"

Liz groaned.

"Sue!"

We gaped at him.

"The point is people make up lawyer jokes because they hate lawyers."

I couldn't help but think Perry was obfuscating (a skill at which lawyers excelled).

The issue wasn't clouded for Anarchy. "There's a difference between hating someone's profession and hating them personally."

Half the people we knew were lawyers. Perry included. And we still liked them.

Anarchy crossed his arms. Somehow, he managed a certain gravitas despite the shorts and cowboy boots combination. "Did Graham have any enemies?"

"You asked that this morning," Perry replied. "My answer hasn't changed.

"So you don't know anyone with a reason to want him dead?"

I gave Perry a silent nudge. *Tell him about the client.*

"Nope. Not a soul."

"I like this barn." I stared up at the rafters. "It's airy. I wonder if they could use it to dry tobacco." I was about as subtle as a jackhammer.

Anarchy stared at me as if I'd suddenly lost my mind.

Perry tugged at his collar and gave me a look best described as a stink-eye.

Liz paled.

Nester whinnied.

I crossed my fingers. *Tell him about the client, Perry. Don't make me do it for you.*

"It's not a motive for murder, but Graham and I had a disagreement about a client."

I released a breath I didn't realize I was holding.

"Oh?" Anarchy shot a suspicious glance my way, then focused his attention on Perry.

"I brought the client into the firm, but Graham took over as lead counsel."

"How did that happen?" I asked.

"Graham snuck onto a plane, flew to North Carolina, and wined and dined them behind Perry's back. The man was a snake." Liz clapped her hand to her mouth and stared at us with wide eyes.

Perry held up his hands. "Be that as it may, I didn't kill him."

"Then who did?" Anarchy didn't expect an answer. He wanted to see how Perry would respond.

"That's your job to figure out." Perry held out his hand to his wife. "Let's go, sweetheart. Our duty is done, and we're supposed to meet Mel and Fred at the dock."

Anarchy waited until they left the barn, then asked, "Was that one of the motives you found this morning?"

"Yes."

"I can't wait to hear the others."

Oh, joy. "When you asked him for an alternative suspect, Perry didn't throw anyone under the bus."

"He did not."

"You've got to respect that. And he told you about the client."

Anarchy's eyes twinkled. "He might have had some prompting. Still, I can't help but like the guy. I hope he's innocent."

I did, too.

CHAPTER SIX

I spread a beach towel on a chaise lounge and plopped myself down next to a pool the size and shape of a postage stamp. Its concrete apron had all the charm of an abandoned quarry. It was still better than swimming in the lake.

"You're really going to stay here?" Libba frowned her disapproval.

I opened the Tab I'd brought with me and sipped. "I am."

"But everyone else is at the lake." Libba wore a red bikini. An expensive red bikini that made my low-cut one-piece suit seem matronly. Libba would regret wearing that suit when she couldn't get rid of the smell of lake water.

"You don't have to stay with me. Go to the lake."

"But you'll be here alone."

"I'm aware." I pointed at the latest issue of *Vogue*. "I'll be fine."

"Why won't you come?"

I regarded her from over the rim of my sunglasses. "Snakes." Also, I needed some time alone.

"There are no snakes."

"You don't know that. If I saw a cottonmouth, it wouldn't have to bite me. I'd have a heart attack in the water and drown."

"You're being ridiculous."

"Go." I shooshed my free hand at her. "I'm going to stay next to the snake-free pool and read this article about *A Chorus Line*." I flipped pages until I found it. "Maybe Anarchy and I will get tickets the next time we go to New York. Look here." I tapped the next page. "There's also an article about Matisse."

"You're the only woman I know who takes *Vogue* for the articles."

I paid attention to the fashion, too. "Matisse was a genius."

Libba, who was unimpressed with dead artists, rolled her eyes. "You're sure you're okay?"

"I'm fine. Go."

"You know there's a killer."

How could I forget? "I found the body."

"There could be a second murder."

"You're worried about me? Don't. Someone wanted Graham dead." A lot of people wanted Graham dead. "I'm not a target."

"What if you're wrong?"

"I'd rather face a man with a gun than a snake."

"Where's Anarchy?"

"Investigating the murder."

She narrowed her eyes.

"He and one of the deputies are searching for the gun."

She cast her eyes back toward the row of cabins. "They're searching our things?"

"Everyone gave their permission." According to Anarchy, getting that permission had been like pulling teeth.

"I can't change your mind?"

"You cannot."

She turned away. The set of her shoulders told me she was unhappy.

"Libba?"

She looked back.

"Thanks for caring."

"Always." With a final, unhappy frown, she left me in peace.

I stretched and enjoyed the sun's rays on my limbs. My eyes closed and the cicadas' soporific drone lulled me. I let my mind wander, and whenever it brushed against murder, I set it in another direction. The fall fashions on the pages of my magazine. Boots. The painting I was working on in my studio. Anarchy's smile first thing in the morning.

"Mind if I join you?"

I opened my eyes.

Buffy stood to the left of my chaise. She had a pool bag over her shoulder, a book under her arm, and an enormous pair of extra-dark sunglasses perched on her nose. Like me she wore a one-piece swimsuit. Hers was yellow with a Kelly green, white, and sienna ribbon pattern. It also had a skirt.

"Please." I gestured to the empty chaise next to me. "What are you reading?"

"*The Moneychangers.* I know people in Shaker Heights."

I doubted her friends were in Hailey's book. "How's Sumner?"

"Resting. I gave her a few Valium." She glanced toward the row of cabins. "And I want to stay close by in case she needs me. The pool is just a stone's throw away. Why are you here?"

"As opposed to the lake?"

She nodded.

"Water snakes."

She shuddered. "I didn't think of the snakes. A second reason to be at the pool."

We shared a moment of understanding, then I asked, "How's Sumner?"

"Her ankle is fine. She barely twisted it."

"Did she say anything about Graham?"

"Not really. I think she's in shock. Any normal woman would be. I mean he was struck down in cold blood."

Given that I'd run over my late husband's body without

going into shock, I couldn't agree with her normal woman assessment. I raised my brows.

"Oh my gracious." She pressed her hand to her lips. "I just realized about Henry. But Sumner's situation is different. You and Henry were…" Buffy searched for a polite way to say my husband was openly cheating on me.

Not that I cared to be reminded.

"Of course you weren't in shock. After the way he treated you, you probably wanted him dead."

My brows rose higher. "When Henry died, I worried about Grace's feelings not my own." I borrowed Mother's best mind-yourself voice—the one that had me correct my posture, fold my hands in my lap, and agree with almost anything she said.

"That came out wrong, and I swallowed my whole foot. Of course you worried for your sweet girl. I'm sorry." She shifted her attention to the tiny square of water. "Anyway, what I should have said is that Sumner and Graham worked out their problems and were on firm footing."

"Their problems?"

Buffy propped her book on her knees and opened the pages. I waited. Hoping.

She winced and as if she were fighting an internal battle, then leaned toward me and whispered, "Graham had an affair."

That did not surprise me. "Anyone we know?"

"No one seems to know who she was—one of the secretaries or paralegals at his firm. It's over now."

Was it? "You're sure?"

"I am. Sumner told me all about it. They went to counseling." I couldn't argue with her source. "When did this happen?"

"Last year. But that's a guess. You know Sumner, she plays close to the vest." Buffy waved at the hot, humid air. "How's marriage treating you? It must be fun to be a newlywed again."

I took another sip of Tab. "Couldn't be happier."

"I must say, your husband asks very direct questions." By

which she meant, he's a nosy-parker, who needs to mind his own business.

"It is a murder investigation." I kept my voice mild.

"I know. I know. He's doing his job. But I was asleep when the murder happened. I have nothing to tell."

"Then answering his questions should be easy."

"Hmph." She opened her book.

I picked up my magazine.

Silence fell.

I hated uncomfortable silence, and, despite her foot-in-mouth disease, I liked Buffy. "What happened last night after I left?"

"You mean after your handsome new husband rescued you from a snake, swept you into his arms, and carried you off into the night?"

She made an embarrassing situation sound like a scene from a romance novel. "Yes. That."

"The caterer and her staff cleaned up the table, replenished the bar, and left."

"No staff?"

"The bartender stayed."

Had Anarchy talked to him? Given all the drinking everyone else did, he might have the clearest picture of what had actually happened last night.

"Wait. I'm wrong. The caterer didn't leave right away. I remember because Graham told her it was the best pineapple upside-down cake he'd ever had, and I caught the expression on Sumner's face."

"She wasn't pleased?"

"Nope."

Presumably Sumner also made pineapple upside-down cake.

"Bill and I spent most of the evening talking to Mel and Fred. Bill and Fred do business together."

Bill made widgets—not really, but I could never remember what Bill actually manufactured. Something about parts that were parts of other parts that went into cars. I'd sat next to him at a dinner party and he'd talked endlessly about how the EPA's requirements and catalytic converters would make our air cleaner. I was all for cleaner air. He lost me on the engineering side.

Fred was a banker with a reputation for making aggressive loans (as a rule, bankers were a conservative sort).

"Bill's business has grown these past few years. And with GM putting catalytic converters in all its cars, there's talk of taking the company public."

"That's wonderful."

Her smile was proud. "Isn't it?"

"Congratulations."

"That's why Bill can't take off for vacation in August. There's too much work. Please, don't tell anyone. It's supposed to be confidential."

I nodded but made no promises. There was a good chance I'd tell Anarchy. "Understood."

"Oh! Merit and Graham argued."

"How did that start?"

"She has her panties in a twist because President Ford was appointed, not elected. She doesn't think he should be treated as an incumbent."

"But he's the President."

"That's what Graham told her. Then she started a diatribe about the Founding Fathers' intent. Deadly dull. Graham suggested she learned her American history from watching *1776*. Well, you know Merit. She has some esoteric degree from Vassar, and his casting aspersions on her education made her spitting mad."

"I can imagine."

"She told Graham he was just a money-grubbing lawyer."

Which lined up with what Libba told me. "What was Tommy doing?"

"Drinking. Steadily. He wanted no part of Merit's little debate. Not even after Graham told her she had a stick up her keister. When she saw her husband wasn't going to fight her battle, she ran off."

"Alone?"

"No one went after her."

Giving her the opportunity to steal Perry's gun. "What did Tommy say?"

"Nothing much. The poor man looked miserable. Bill changed the subject to baseball."

"What do you think the problem is?"

"With Merit and Tommy?"

I nodded. The answer was obvious, but I was interested in Buffy's take.

"I want your opinion, too. You take Merit."

"Merit cloaks her insecurities in airs." It was more than that. As long as Merit defined herself as the smartest person in the room, she could pretend emotions didn't matter. By poking fun at her knowledge and intelligence, Graham had attacked her sense of self.

Buffy nodded her agreement, then said, "Tommy went to Harvard, but he's never done a thing but marry Merit and run her family's company. He's bored and frustrated and tired." Her assessment was spot on.

"He's a nice man."

"The nicest," she agreed.

By which we meant that it was a crying shame he was wasting his life saddled with a woman who needed to feel intellectually and morally superior to everyone she met.

Of course, we didn't say that. Not out loud. But we thought it.

Buffy stared into the near distance. "Liz and Perry danced. So did Libba and Charlie."

"And after the singer left?"

"We sat around the table and talked."

"Did anyone else leave?"

"Mel and I visited the ladies' room in the clubhouse together. Sumner went, too. She came back claiming she'd seen a raccoon on the path."

"The men?"

"I don't remember. You probably heard that Charlie and Graham had words."

"I did. What precipitated the argument?"

"Thatch said something about billable hours, and Graham said he had him beat by a country mile. That's when Charlie mentioned the lawsuit. He asked if the only thing Graham cared about was billing hours."

"What was Graham's response?"

"He said he also cared about winning cases. Then, Charlie called him a weasel and said that men like him always got their comeuppance."

"And?"

"Graham asked if that was a threat."

"What did Charlie say?"

"Libba pulled him away. Thatch made a joke. And we all laughed. The moment was over."

That was within in spitting distance of the story Libba and Charlie had told me.

A drop of sweat rolled off my nose, and I stood and took off my glasses. "Hold that thought." I jumped into the pool.

"How's the water?"

"Too warm." Almost bathwater.

"The lake is probably cooler."

Undoubtedly. "Two words. Water moccasins."

Buffy held up her hands. "You don't need to convince me. I will never dip a toe in that water."

I sank below the surface and held my breath for a few seconds. When I emerged, droplets sparkled on my lashes, and the world seemed cooler.

I dove under again, touched the bottom of the pool, and did a handstand. I was behaving like a child on the first day of pool season and I didn't care. The water washed away my worries and I felt lighter.

Finally, I broke the surface for air.

"Do you still swim in the morning?" Buffy asked.

"I do. Anarchy comes with me."

She nodded. "You look good. Fit. Toned."

"Thank you. I try." I pushed out of the pool just as Mel Paige approached.

"Ellison, I've been looking for you."

"Oh?" Did she want to complain about Anarchy, too?

"Will you shoot skeet with me? Please?"

"Now?" It was bone-meltingly hot.

"The alternative is puttering around the lake." She made it sound so boring she might die.

"You could join us here at the pool."

Mel did not look impressed by my suggestion.

"We can go shooting later, Mel."

"When?"

I randomly picked a time. "Seven o'clock?"

"That's hours away."

"Go with her," Buffy urged. "You know how she gets." Once Mel got an idea in her head, it was near impossible to change it.

"It's hot," I complained.

"You can swim after we shoot. The water will be twice as refreshing."

The water wasn't terribly refreshing now. A few more hours of sunlight would not improve its temperature.

"Please?" Mel hit me with puppy-dog eyes.

I knew Mel. She wouldn't stop asking. Not until she wore me down. "Fine. Give me a few minutes to change."

"Great. Thank you! I'll meet you at the range."

Fifteen minutes later, wearing jean shorts, cowboy boots (because, snakes) and a long-sleeved t-shirt, I joined Mel at the field.

The guys moving into the trap houses looked even less than thrilled to be there than I was. I couldn't hold their thunderous expressions against them, the heat in the tiny boxes had to be awful.

Mel shot her way around the circle and only missed three clays. "Your turn. What are we shooting for?"

"A cold beer in the shade."

"When?"

"Right after my round. It's too hot for this."

She tilted her head. "Since when are you a delicate flower?"

"I was thinking about the guys in the trap houses. They have to be melting."

"Oh. Right." She frowned. "I didn't think about them."

I picked up a shotgun, wiped the sweat from my eyes, and hit every clay. "That's it, guys," I called. "You can come out."

The two men, positively dripping with sweat, emerged from the trap houses. I gave them each slightly damp twenty dollars from my back pocket, then turned to Mel. "You owe me that beer." And shade. I wanted shade almost as much as I wanted a cold beverage.

"A deal's a deal." She didn't look happy about it. "There's beer in the fridge at our cabin."

"Lead the way."

I followed her to the cabin closest to the clubhouse. There was a view of the lake and the gazebo. When we stepped inside, I found the same rustic charm, the same knotty pine, and an actual sitting area. "This is nice."

"Compared to what? Have a seat."

I collapsed onto a loveseat covered in a deeply ugly, nubby, plaid fabric. Who thought harvest gold, burnt sienna, avocado green, and puke brown (Anarchy could attest to the accuracy of that shade) went together?

"Do you want a glass?"

"Yes, please."

Mel took two mugs from the freezer and two beers from the fridge, then gave me one of each.

I poured my drink and shifted on the lumpy couch. The fabric was scratchy against the back of my thighs and I suspected there was a spring loose.

Mel took the seat across from me, poured her beer, and drank. "I have to admit, this is a good idea."

"It's brutal out there." The beer mug was so cold it hurt my hands. I clasped it tighter. "You shot well."

"You beat me."

I sipped my beer and shifted again. The couch's springs could serve as torture devices.

"How are you doing? It must have been terrible finding Graham." That was unusually empathetic for Mel.

"It was horrifying."

"I've hunted all my life, but I can't imagine what he must have looked like."

Perhaps less empathetic, more ghoulish.

"Your husband asks clear concise questions." She wasn't complaining, which was refreshing. "Of course, Fred and I were sleeping when Graham was shot."

The heat had sapped my strength, so much so I was willing to ignore the spring and lean back against the couch. "Of course."

"We stayed up too late. Fred was supposed to fish this morning. He promised to wake Graham, but the alarm didn't go off. If it had, Fred might have found him."

"What time were they supposed to go?"

She took another long sip. "Five thirty."

"Early."

She nodded. "It's not like Fred to forget to set his alarm. But I'm glad he did." She finished the last of her beer. "Would you like another?"

My glass was half-full. "No, thank you."

"I want one." She stood, took a bottle from the fridge, and poured the beer into her glass. "I can't help but think of Sumner. A widow so young. Then, you were a young widow."

"I was."

"In some ways her life may be easier now."

I sat up straight. "How so?"

"Sumner can't balance a checkbook to save her life. Fred had to call Graham several times a month to transfer funds."

The spring dug into my cheek, and I scooched to the far end of the cushion.

"In a way, it was Graham's fault. He gave her a tiny allowance. Now she can have more than a pittance." She stared into her glass and frowned. "I shouldn't be telling you that."

Why was she? Was it even true?

"Did you and Fred bring guns this weekend?"

"We did." She nodded toward a shotgun case.

"Handguns?"

She turned the glass in her hands. "Why do you ask?"

"Just wondering? I was talking with someone about guns earlier today. I assumed everyone brought a handgun."

"Not us."

The darned spring. I shifted again.

"Is something wrong with your seat?"

"It's a bit lumpy. The club should invest in a new couch."

"We can plump the cushion."

"I doubt that will help."

"We'll never know unless we try. Get up."

I stood, and Mel yanked the cushion off the couch.

We both stared. At a gun.

"You said you didn't bring a handgun."

"That's not mine."

"Is it Fred's?"

"Fred doesn't own a Luger".

"That's a Luger?"

She reached for the gun.

"Don't touch that!"

She jerked her hand away. "Why not?"

"It's probably the murder weapon."

CHAPTER SEVEN

*A*narchy and I took cover beneath the spreading limbs of an oak tree not far from Mel and Fred's cabin. The sheriff's deputy, who looked to be only a few years older than Grace, huddled in the shade with us. He held the top edge of a plastic bag. Inside the bag was the gun I'd found in Mel's couch. The Luger looked ugly. Not a showpiece, but a deadly weapon.

Perry had taken one quick look at the gun and given a grim nod. The gun belonged to him.

His pale-faced admission had made a bad day worse. My heart ached for Sumner, my shoulder ached from too much shooting, and my stomach churned with worry for Liz and Perry/

Despite the oak's shade, the heat did its best to burn us to a crisp. I waved at stifling air perfumed by the aroma of meat in a smoker and gave silent thanks it wasn't my job to manage coals.

The sheriff's deputy, whose name was Cole Harden, asked, "Will there be anything else, Detective Jones?"

"Just get the weapon processed. Maybe we'll get lucky and find fingerprints."

I, for one, didn't think we'd be lucky enough to find any prints but Perry's.

"On it." Deputy Harden nodded a goodbye, then trudged toward the parking lot.

Anarchy wiped his brow with his forearm. "Tell me how Mel reacted when you found the gun."

"She was shocked."

"Acting?"

I considered his question. "I don't think so. She swayed, and I thought she'd fall." Mel had grabbed a chair back to remain standing.

He scowled at the leaves protecting us from the scorching sky. "Deputy Harden searched their cabin earlier today, and he swears the weapon wasn't there."

"Why Mel and Fred's cabin? Is someone trying to frame them? Why didn't the killer toss the gun into the woods, where you might never find it?"

Mel and Fred had the first of eight cabins. Buffy and Bill had the second. Then came Merit and Tommy. After them, came Libba and Charlie and Willa and Thatch. Liz and Perry were next. Anarchy and I were in the seventh. Sumner and Graham had been in the eighth.

The club manager kept a small apartment in the clubhouse. The catering staff were housed in a lodge near the lake that was hardly habitable. Thus far, Misty and her people hadn't complained.

Anarchy rubbed his chest, as if the whole situation was giving him heartburn. "I don't know. And, I have to wonder if Harden missed the gun when he searched."

"The gun wasn't well hidden." My bottom could attest to that.

I wiped sweat from my hairline. "It's so hot, I can't think."

"Why don't you go back to the cabin? The air conditioner might be loud, but at least it's cool.

"Good idea."

"What the…"

I followed Anarchy's worried gaze.

Randy approached us at a dead run. He pulled up when he reached the shade, then bent over as if couldn't breathe. The man was ruddy at the best of times. Running in the heat had turned his skin a deep red. He drew a rasping breath, then gasped, "Sorry to interrupt, but there's a call for you, Mrs. Jones."

"For me?"

Randy straightened, grimaced, and ran his palm across the back of his boiled-lobster neck. "It's your mother."

We let that horror sink in.

"I told her it might take a while to find you. She said she'd wait."

She would, too. She'd hold the line, growing increasingly annoyed with each passing minute. I pictured her at her desk with her white hair sprayed into a perfect helmet. She was probably picking an imaginary piece of lint from the sleeve of her St. John dress. That, or tapping a perfectly manicured nail on the blotter. Waiting. For me. I glanced at my husband. "I'd better take this." *Please, please, think of a reason I shouldn't.*

Anarchy offered me a rueful smile. He knew what Mother was like. He knew she was unavoidable, like death, taxes, or lost socks in the dryer.

We both knew why she was calling.

How bad could this day get?

I girded my loins and followed Randy to the clubhouse.

Anne Boleyn, on her way to meet the axe, walked with more enthusiasm than I did.

We reached the building and stepped into the air-conditioning. I paused and let the sudden cool coat my skin.

"She's waiting." Randy pointed to a small office, then ran as if Mother were a character from *The Exorcist*.

I nodded and ventured inside.

Randy's office featured knotty pine paneling, a battered desk covered with ledgers and hunting magazines, a calendar featuring a German shorthair pointing in a field tacked to the wall, plaid curtains at the windows, and a braided rag rug on the worn floor. I breathed deep, held the blessedly cool air in my lungs for ten whole seconds, then exhaled slowly. The exercise did nothing to calm my nerves. With a shaking hand, I picked up the receiver and briefly considered returning it to its cradle.

She'd call back, even more annoyed. Or, worse, she'd get in her car and drive down here.

"Hello." I tried to sound upbeat, as if I was pleased to hear from her.

"Do you know how long I've been waiting? It's long distance, Ellison. This call is costing me a fortune."

"You could have left a message." An entirely reasonable suggestion.

One which she ignored. "Tell me it isn't true."

"It isn't true," I deadpanned.

"Don't sass me." Who needed air-conditioning? Mother's voice was cold enough to bring on the next ice age.

This call was off to a bang-up start. "What do you want to hear, Mother?"

"Did you, or did you not, find Graham Landingham's body this morning?"

"Strictly speaking, Sumner and I found him together."

"You can't make it one weekend without tripping over a corpse?"

"I didn't trip." I'd stood in the doorway and absorbed the horror. "Who told you?"

"Never you mind."

Someone had called Kansas City, called a friend or a loved one, and told them about Graham.

Given how gossip worked, I was surprised it took as long as it did for Mother to call me.

"When will you be home?" she demanded. Apparently, she was eager for the opportunity to excoriate me in person.

"I don't know. Anarchy is investigating the murder."

"No," she corrected. "Anarchy is investigating your friends. I warned you this would happen."

She had warned me. On multiple occasions.

I sank into the beat-up leather chair behind the desk. "It's his job, Mother."

"And you aren't bothered that your husband is digging into your friends' lives?"

"In a perfect world—"

"It's not a perfect world, Ellison."

I was well aware. "Someone murdered Graham. Police ask questions in a murder investigation. It doesn't matter if it's Anarchy or another detective, someone will ask those questions."

"Do you honestly think Bill Geller will want to play golf with Anarchy after he exposes the man's sordid affairs?"

Anarchy had no desire to play golf. And, if he did, he'd play with me, not Bill. "Unless Bill killed Graham, Anarchy won't expose anything."

"Don't be obtuse. Anarchy will know. And Bill will know he knows."

How could I argue with logic like that? I had to try. "Mother, everyone knows about Bill's affairs."

"Do you think Fred Paige will ask Anarchy for drinks if he exposes the problems at Fred's bank?"

I blinked. "What problems?"

"He made a bad loan."

"One bad loan? It must have been a whopper."

"Don't change the subject. Anarchy won't be asked for drinks."

"Anarchy can live happily without meeting Fred Paige for cocktails."

"What's more, no one appreciates being forced to stay there." It was as if she didn't hear a word I said.

"The sheriff requested that everyone stay, not Anarchy. Besides, we all planned on being here through tomorrow."

"That was before Graham's murder. People want the safety of their homes. Especially when there could be a raving, gun-toting lunatic rampaging through the woods."

Seriously? That was the best she could do? "I doubt there's a lunatic in the woods."

"Don't take that tone with me."

"Don't conjure crazed killers. Someone killed Graham for a reason." A crazed killer wouldn't hide his gun beneath the sofa cushions in Mel and Fred's cabin. He'd keep the gun and shoot more people. "Tell me more about Fred's bank."

"So you can tell your husband?"

Yes. Exactly. "Does Fred have a motive to kill Graham?

She was quiet for so long I dared hope we'd lost our connection.

"Your father mentioned something." Her admission was reluctant.

"Oh?"

"Graham took one of his clients to Fred for a loan. Graham vouched for the man."

"Does that mean he co-signed the note?"

She barked a laugh. "No. Not remotely. Fred made the loan, and six weeks later, the man was bankrupt. Your father says the man's legal bills were paid in full before he filed for bankruptcy with courts."

Had Graham known? Had he arranged the loan so he could be paid, then left Fred holding the bag? If that wasn't malpractice, it was at least an ethics violation. "I bet Fred was furious." Except, at no time during the weekend had he seemed angry.

I glanced out the window and spotted Misty standing next to a smoker the size of a small Honda. During Kansas City summers, barbeque was a way of life. Texas and Memphis and the Carolinas claimed the best barbeque, but they were wrong. Texans only cooked beef. The folks in Tennessee, who loved their dry rubs, didn't understand sauces. And in the Carolinas, cooks favored pork. Only Kansas City did everything well.

"Ellison, are you there?"

"Sorry. I drifted." The heat had cooked too many brain cells. "You were saying?"

"Fred is absolutely furious. A bank examiner has taken over his conference room."

"Mel hasn't said a thing."

"Can you blame her? Do you air your dirty laundry in public?"

"No."

"Yet, you think your friends want to share theirs with your husband?"

Obviously, Fred's dirty laundry wasn't as secret as he might hope. "Daddy can't be the only one who knows about Fred's bank."

"That's beside the point."

"So, you're worried Anarchy will discover poorly kept secrets?"

"Your new husband has plenty of faults, but stupidity isn't one of them. He'll discover their secrets. My worry is that your friends will blame you when he does."

I thought it best not to mention that I was as good at ferreting out secrets as my husband. "I'll survive."

"You say that now. Just wait until you're dropped from a committee." That wasn't much of a threat. "Or until Grace is excluded because Anarchy turned over too many rocks."

That gave me pause. Grace had wanted justice when her

father was murdered. Surely, she'd want justice for Graham. "I'll discuss it with her."

"Your father had lunch with Wright Gibson yesterday."

"Oh?" Where was she going with this? Wright ran the largest bank in the region, and I couldn't imagine he had anything to do with Graham's death.

"He has an opening for a vice-president of security."

I should have guessed. "Anarchy likes being a homicide detective. I'd never ask him to give up his career."

"Has he considered sitting for the captain's exam?"

My husband didn't want an administrative role. "He likes solving murders."

"Ellison, be reasonable." She was the one being unreasonable. "Wright wants Anarchy to call him when you're back in town."

Sometimes it was easier not to argue. As I aged, I was becoming increasingly adept at not arguing with Mother while still getting my own way. "I'll let him know."

"Good. In the meantime, see if you can't keep him from destroying relationships you've cherished for decades."

"This call is costing you a fortune." Not arguing. Just using her own words against her. I eased the receiver closer to the cradle. "I'll talk to you when I'm back in town. Goodbye." I hung up before she could object, then I sat and thought.

Mother and Daddy were meddling. Why was I surprised?

Randy peeked into the office. "Everything okay?"

"Fine. Thank you."

"Your mother is a forceful woman." He didn't know the half of it. Mother was an F5 tornado in human form. Randy rubbed his chin. "You gave Pug and Jepp twenty-dollar tips."

"Is that a problem?"

"No. Not at all. It was nice of you."

"I felt awful for dragging them out in that heat."

"Not everyone's so considerate."

"They work hard."

He grinned at me. "You need anything, you let me know."

"May I make another call?"

He waved at the ancient black telephone. "Help yourself."

I waited until Randy left, then dialed home.

"Jones' residence." Aggie, our housekeeper, answered the phone. I imagined my housekeeper standing in our air-conditioned kitchen with a glass of fresh-made iced tea nearby. In my mind, she wore a cotton kaftan, one with cobalt blue birds soaring across a cadmium green background, dangly earrings, and a wrist stacked with bangles.

"Aggie, it's me."

"Are you having a nice weekend?" Her voice was warm and caring.

"I found a body."

She laughed.

I didn't.

She caught herself. "You mean it?"

"I'm afraid so. Is Grace home?"

"I'm sorry, she's not. She went to the Plaza with friends. Who died?"

"A man named Graham Landingham."

"Is his wife called Sumner?"

"Yes. You know them?"

"I know their housekeeper, Bernie. What happened to Mr. Landingham?"

"He was shot."

She inhaled sharply. "Oh, my gracious."

"Anarchy is investigating. We may not make it home tomorrow."

"I understand. I'll keep an eye on Grace. And Max."

"He's not causing you any trouble?"

"No more than usual." With Max, that could mean treeing cats, raiding the pantry, or chewing through the handles of all my purses. "He has his lady love to keep him happy." Max and

Charlie's golden were soulmates. Together, they could destroy whole blocks. "They're nothing I can't handle."

"Thank you, Aggie."

"My pleasure. If I happen to talk to Bernie, I'll let you know."

If she happened to talk to Bernie? Knowing Aggie, that conversation was a certainty. "Again, thank you."

"Is there anything else I can do?"

"Just tell Grace I called. I'm thinking of her."

"I'll tell her." She hung up the phone.

I left Randy's office, and Bear, the club Labrador who spent his days sprawled in front of the fireplace in the lounge, lifted his head and grinned.

I knelt and scratched behind his ears. "Who's a good boy?"

His tail whacked the floor, and he gazed at me with adoring eyes.

"How bad was it?" Anarchy had come to find me.

"Not good."

He crouched next to me and let Bear sniff his hand. "She's worried your friends will hold my investigation against you."

"How did you know?"

"I worry about the same thing."

"Don't. I married you knowing what you do for a living." I watched Anarchy scratch beneath Bear's graying chin. "Mother wants you to call Wright Gibson when we're back in Kansas City."

"Who?"

"He's a banker."

Anarchy tilted his head and frowned. "And?"

"He's looking for someone to run security for his regional bank."

"I see."

"You don't have to call."

"But?"

"But nothing. I don't want you to change. Not for me. Certainly not for Mother."

His expression softened. "I love you."

"I love you, too."

Magic hung in the air around us. This was real and true and perfect and—

Bear passed gas, almost as bad as Tommy's.

We scrambled off the floor with our eyes watering and took giant steps away from the still grinning dog.

"Can we solve this thing quickly so Mother will leave me alone?"

"I'm trying."

"I know you are. It would be easier if everyone here didn't have a motive."

"Everyone?" He looked at me expectantly.

"I haven't found a motive for Buffy, Bill, or Tommy. But the day's not over. Oh. I forgot Libba. She had no reason to kill Graham.

He rubbed his chin and nodded. "Okay, then. Let's talk this through."

I straightened my shoulders. "Chances are the killer used Perry's gun."

"Agreed."

"Perry had a reason to want Graham dead."

"I know."

I threw out another name. "Thatch."

"The managing partner role?"

"Yep."

"Was Graham in serious contention?" asked Anarchy.

"I'll ask Liz. Charlie had a motive. Then there's Fred."

"Fred?"

I repeated what Mother told me about the loan. "There's also Sumner. You always look at the spouse."

"I do."

"He had an affair. Buffy says it ended."

"You look as if you have more to say."

"Aggie knows their housekeeper, Bernie. If she happens to speak with her—"

Anarchy chuckled. "If?"

"When," I ceded.

Bear made a sound like an outboard motor, and Anarchy claimed my arm. "Let's get out of here."

We stepped onto the front porch and squinted in the sun. Anarchy pulled out a pair of aviator sunglasses and I put on my wayfarers.

The outdoors was an oven. "It's hot."

He nodded. "Why don't you go to the cabin and rest in the air-conditioning?"

"Where are you going?"

"I have a call to make, then I have a few questions for Mel and Fred."

"I bet. Motive. No real alibis. And the gun found in their cabin. Although, I think someone planted that gun."

"It's possible." He leaned down and brushed a kiss across my lips. "I'll see you soon."

"It's a date."

"Be careful."

"I always am."

He chuckled. "We both know that's not true."

CHAPTER EIGHT

I left Anarchy in the clubhouse and walked toward the cabins. First came Mel and Fred's. Then Buffy and Bill's, where an enormous oak cast shade over the clearing. How was Sumner? And why was the cabin's door half-way open?

Should I bother her?

The poor woman deserved some privacy, but leaving a door open was like air-conditioning the outside.

I hesitated.

Intruding on her grief was wrong, but hadn't she heard of the energy crisis?

Decision made, I stepped onto the porch and knocked gently.

Sumner didn't answer.

I peered through the screen door and saw two sets of bunk beds, knotty pine paneling, a couch similar to the one in Mel and Fred's cabin, and a breakfast table surrounded by four ladder-back chairs.

No sign of Sumner. Where was she?

"Sumner?"

No one replied. The cabin was empty. I frowned, pulled the

door closed, and returned to the path, zig-gagging between trees to stay in the shade.

When I reached our cabin, I poked my head inside. The window unit sounded like a jet at take-off. Hardly restful. Hardly conducive to figuring out who killed Graham. I couldn't stay here, not when the site of a murder was a mere hundred-fifty feet away. Not when questions scrolled through my head.

I walked on, rounded the bend to the last cabin, and spotted Sumner. She stood on the front porch, fingering the police tape that blocked her access to the cabin where her husband died.

Sumner and I weren't close—she was eight years younger than me and seemed bored by talk of children or art. Then there was the whole eyelash issue. But watching her, I felt a moment's empathy. I understood exactly what she was going through.

"Sumner?"

She turned at my voice. She still wore her running clothes, but she'd taken off her eyelashes. Without the spiders on her eyelids, she looked younger. More approachable and real. Maybe even prettier. And that was despite the redness and puffiness that surrounded her baby blues.

Not an observation she'd appreciate. "How are you doing?"

She shook her head, and her limp ponytail barely bounced. "I can't believe he's gone."

"I'm sorry for your loss."

Her lips thinned, and she beat her fisted hands against her upper thighs. "I told him we shouldn't come this weekend. I told him again and again. But he wouldn't listen, he insisted."

"May I ask, why did you come? Most everyone here seems to have been angry with him. It couldn't have been comfortable."

She snorted. "For whom?"

"For you. For Graham." For anyone with reason to hate him.

"Graham didn't care about their anger."

Look what that got him.

She pressed the heel of her hand to her forehead. "You heard about his argument with Charlie?"

"I did."

"And Merit?"

"Her, too."

"Graham could be such an idiot. I told him this was a bad idea. But he'd made up his mind." She grabbed the ends of her ponytail and tightened it. "Staying home would have looked like hiding, like weakness."

"Who invited you?"

She grimaced. "Willa called."

I shifted so that I stood in deeper shade.

"You're wondering why I told him about the invitation. I could have declined, and he would have never known."

The thought had crossed my mind. I gave a tiny shrug.

"I didn't tell him. Our housekeeper took a message, and he saw it before I did." She pressed a knuckl to her teeth and let out a raspy sob. "If I'd arrived home before he did, things would be different. We wouldn't be here." Tears welled in her eyes. "He wouldn't be dead."

"You can't blame yourself. Guilt falls firmly on whoever killed him."

"Who killed him? Half the people here were angry with him."

An understatement. "It does seem that way."

"There's Thatch and the whole managing partner thing, the issue with Fred's bank, the argument with Charlie, the spat with Perry, and the issue with Bill."

"What issue with Bill?" That was new.

"Bill would have gotten over it. Eventually."

"What was Bill mad about?"

"I'm not exactly sure. But Graham told me Bill was furious with him. Something to do with the management of his company and the stock offering."

I added Bill to the list of people with motives. "I still don't

understand why Graham wanted to spend the weekend with
people who were mad at him." Maybe even hated him.

"You know how men are." She waited for me to respond.
When I didn't, she continued. "Graham never backed down
from a fight. Not once. It was a point of honor for him."

"That couldn't have been fun to live with."

Her answering chuckle was dark. "It was not. It did make
him a good lawyer."

But not a good person.

"Don't ever hire a nice lawyer." She shook her head at all the
saps who hired decent human beings. "If you need an attorney,
you want a pit bull, not a cocker spaniel."

If I hired an attorney, I wanted one with integrity. "I'll keep
that in mind."

"That's what people didn't understand. It was never personal
for Graham. It was about getting the best result for his client."
She sniffed and wiped her eyes. "And winning."

"I see." I didn't. Not really. I'd rather lose with honor than
bend rules or step on people to win.

Sumner scraped her fingers through her hair. "What did you
do after your husband died? How did you…"

"How did I manage? I ran. I grabbed my daughter and
hopped on a plane for Europe."

"Did it help?"

"Yes, and no. Europe gave us some distance. But we still had
to process our grief." Grace more than me. "Henry and I weren't
on firm footing when he died. I was more worried about my
daughter than my sadness."

"I don't know if having children would make this easier or
harder. I can't imagine what you went through—comforting a
child after her father's murder."

I didn't have an answer to that. Grace had adored her father
and losing him would be a lifelong wound.

Sumner rubbed a hand across her face. "I wanted children,

but it never happened for us." She stared into the woods for long seconds, then straightened her shoulders. "Graham told me not to worry about it. He was already paying two tuitions."

Graham's first wife, Roux, had negotiated an epic divorce settlement. Unhappy wives still talked about it, wondered how she'd ended up so well off. I'd heard Graham was on the hook for tuition as long as his children wanted to be in school, up to and including med school. The two children he had with Roux were entitled to half his estate, no matter how many additional children he had or if he was married at the time of his death. And, until she remarried, Roux had received huge alimony checks.

"I wish I knew who did this."

"Did you see anyone when you were running this morning?"

"Bill and you." She pursed her lips. "I can't believe you didn't hear the gunshot."

"The air-conditioner in our cabin is so loud, someone could have blown up your cabin and we wouldn't have heard a thing."

"When you came outside?"

"If Graham was shot while I was on the path, I'd have heard it." A gunshot would certainly have torn my focus from finding coffee. "I didn't hear a thing but the birds."

She frowned. "Does your husband have a suspect?"

He had too many suspects. "Not that he's told me."

She crossed her arms. "Graham deserves justice."

"Agreed. Anarchy will catch the killer. You just have to give him more than a few hours."

"What about the murder weapon?"

"What about it?"

"Have the police found it?"

"Possibly."

Here brows lifted. "Where?"

"Hidden in one of the cabins."

"Then he's found the killer."

"Not necessarily. The gun could have been planted."

"Planted?" She frowned. "Who would do that" And why?"

"Someone might have put the gun in the cabin to shift the focus from the real killer." I glanced at the yellow tape. "Do you have a theory? Who killed Graham?"

Sumner stared at her feet. "I can't say."

"Can't or won't?"

Her cheeks flushed. "I can't put a friend in your husband's cross-hairs."

"I thought you wanted justice." If she meant that, she'd share her suspicions.

"I do." She joined me in staring at the yellow tape on the door. "But Buffy has been very kind".

Did that mean she thought Bill had killed Graham?

She straightened her shoulders and lifted her chin. "The deputy moved my suitcase to a room in the main clubhouse. I think I'll head that way. I might feel better if I showered." She stepped away from the door, stepped onto the path, and turned her back on me.

"Let me know if you need company."

She paused. "That's very kind of you. Thank you."

I watched her walk away.

"Psst." The whisper came from behind a bush.

My shoulders tightened. "Who's there?"

"Wait a second."

Wait? Wait until Sumner was gone and whoever was hiding could shoot me without a witness? I trotted after Sumner, but she was already out of sight.

"Ellison, hold up." Liz emerged from behind the bush with her hands held high.

"What are you doing? You scared me to death."

"Sorry. I didn't mean to."

"What were you doing back there?"

She smoothed her peasant dress. "I wasn't eavesdropping. I promise. I didn't want to see Sumner. I don't know what to say to her."

"You're sorry for her loss." Sarcasm dripped heavy from my voice.

"I'm not sorry Graham is dead. He was a horrible man."

"You can be sorry that Sumner lost her husband."

"You're right. I should do that." She made offering sympathy sound worse than wading through a pit of vipers.

"But?"

"I will. I will." She rubbed her fingers across her lips.

"But?"

"Fine," she huffed. "I never much liked her."

We were on the same page, but Sumner was obviously grieving. And kindness was always a good thing. "I'm still not clear on why you're hiding in the bushes."

"I told you I didn't want Sumner to see me."

"I get that. But why are you here?"

"I came to find you. To see if you'd drink wine with me."

"Yes. A thousand times, yes."

"Let's go." She linked her arm with mine, and we walked to her cabin, which was exactly like the one I shared with Anarchy. Except, the air-conditioner allowed for conversation.

"White?" She opened the refrigerator and pulled out a bottle.

"Please."

"There's a corkscrew here somewhere." She opened the drawer next to the kitchen sink and rifled through it. "Success." She held up the corkscrew, used it to open the wine, then took two juice glasses from the cabinet, and poured.

"Thank you." I took a glass from her outstretched hand.

"Have a seat."

I pulled a chair away from the table and sank onto it.

She joined me. "We had no idea when we planned this that it would be the hottest weekend of the year."

She could complain about the heat, but Liz looked like she'd stepped into her backyard to pick a few tomatoes. Pleasantly flushed.

I looked like I'd worked a double-shift on a road crew. "It's brutal."

We clinked the rims of our juice glasses, and Liz said, "You've had a day."

I drank. "I have."

"I really wasn't eavesdropping. I promise." She stared into her glass. "I couldn't help but hear Sumner hint that Bill was the killer. Do you think she's right?"

"I have no idea."

"I wonder what she meant about Bill's business."

Liz wanted conjecture. I concentrated on the wine, which was cool and crisp and delicious.

"What else did Sumner say?" she asked.

"Not much."

"She seems genuinely upset."

"Her husband was murdered." I took another sip of wine. "What were the chances of Graham becoming managing partner?"

Liz curled her lip as if her wine had turned sour. "Better than fifty percent."

"Even with the number of people who disliked him?"

"He brought in business." She snorted. "Or stole it."

"You and Willa put this weekend together. Why did Willa ask them?"

"Thatch insisted. He said we needed to be friendly."

"I went shooting with Thatch and Graham yesterday. There was an undercurrent that wasn't friendly."

She nodded. "Not surprising. The two men didn't like each other. They just pretended they did."

"Why bother?"

"They had to work together. Being civil helped with that."

"I see."

"Look, I don't know who killed Graham, but I do know it wasn't Perry or Thatch."

"I understand believing in your husband, but what makes you so sure about Thatch?"

"Willa swears he's innocent."

Thatch had wanted Graham here. He'd insisted. Now Graham was dead. I wasn't nearly as certain of Thatch's innocence as Willa. "This is going to sound awful, but why invite Merit and Tommy?"

She wrinkled her nose. "She can be a lot to take. But Perry and Tommy have been friends for years."

"Tommy seems to be drinking a lot." Like a fish.

"More than a lot. We're worried about him."

"Any idea why?"

"If I had to live with Merit, I'd drink, too."

She made a fair point. I raised my juice glass.

"So, Bill." She took a sip of wine. "Did he do it?"

"He's one of the few people with an actual alibi."

"What about Sumner? Maybe she killed Graham before she went running."

The thought had occurred to me. "It's possible, but what's Sumner's motive?"

"Money?"

I shrugged. "I assume Graham made a decent salary, and that his year-end bonus was sizeable." Liz would know better than I. "His children will get half the estate. And the real wealth is with Graham's parents. Both of whom are still alive. With Graham dead, Sumner will never see a penny of the Landingham fortune."

Liz looked non-plussed. "Who else has an alibi?"

"Everyone, and no one."

"What does that mean?"

"Your Perry's alibi, and he's yours. Would you lie for him?"

She flushed. "I don't have to lie. We were together. Asleep."

"Lizzie." I reached across the table and squeezed her hand. "I don't think you had anything to do with Graham's death." At least I hoped not. "My point is spouses lie for each other."

"What about the staff?"

"Misty was in the kitchen. Both Bill and I saw her. Her helpers were at the lodge."

"Randy?"

"I don't know. I'll ask Anarchy. But as far as I know, Randy and Graham never met before this weekend."

"Buffy! If Bill went fishing, she doesn't have an alibi."

"True. Can you think of a reason Buffy would kill Graham?"

"Maybe that thing with Bill that Sumner hinted at. When I found out what Graham did to Perry, I was mad enough to kill him." She pressed her fingers to her lips. "Not that I did."

"Of course."

She held up the bottle. "More wine?"

"One more glass."

The cabin door opened, and Perry stepped inside. His brows rose when he saw me. "Ellison, good afternoon."

"I'm drinking wine with your wife."

"Smart. I may drink bourbon while you drink wine."

"The boat was that bad?" asked Liz.

"Let's just say murder does not bring out the best in people. Especially when we all suspect each other."

"Ellison and I have been trading theories."

He poured bourbon into a juice glass, then perched on the edge of the bed. "Let's hear them."

"It seems everyone has a motive." Liz sounded almost flippant.

"Bill and Fred, too?"

"Yep." She popped the "p."

"Do tell," said Perry.

"Ellison?" Liz looked at me expectantly.

"I'm in the dark about Bill. There may be some issue with Fred's bank."

They waited for more. When I remained silent, Liz pouted. "That's it? That's all you'll tell us?"

I shrugged. "I don't know much more than that."

"Buffy has no alibi," Liz told her husband.

"Buffy's your suspect?"

"I wouldn't go that far." I kept my voice mild.

"I assumed I was suspect number one. Graham was shot with my gun."

"We don't know that for sure," Liz snapped.

"My gun went missing. Graham was shot with a handgun. Ellison found my gun in Fred and Mel's cabin."

"Exactly, the gun went missing. You couldn't have used it."

"We could be lying."

"Perry! This isn't a joke. Graham was murdered. Stop acting like you enjoy being a suspect."

Perry grinned. "This is the most exciting thing to happen to me in years. Ellison, you understand."

I did. Perry fancied himself the third Hardy Boy. He was enthralled by the mystery, the thrill of the hunt. It was what kept Anarchy at his job. But Perry had lost sight of the dead man. Anarchy never forgot the victims.

"Who do you think killed Graham?" I asked.

"No idea," Perry replied. "Not a random stranger. It was definitely one of us."

"Thatch insisted that Graham be invited."

"Did he?" Now Perry's tone gave nothing away.

I did not, for one second, believe Perry was ignorant of that fact. "Were there any problems between Graham and Thatch, aside from vying for the managing partner job?"

"Not that I'm aware of."

"How long has Thatch been managing partner?"

Perry tilted his head and frowned. "Three or four years."

That long? "You'd think he'd want to step down."

"I know I would," Perry agreed.

"So why not let Graham have a turn?"

"You'd have to ask Thatch."

"More wine?" asked Liz.

My glass was empty a second time. How had that happened? "No, thank you." I stood. "I need to clean up before dinner."

"So you're going?" asked Liz.

"Aren't you?"

She glanced at her husband.

He grinned. "We wouldn't miss it. The killer might crack under pressure and confess."

I wasn't holding my breath on that.

CHAPTER NINE

The mouthwatering scent of pork ribs and slow-smoked brisket lured Anarchy and me to dinner. We arrived at the picnic table at the same time as Liz and Perry and Willa and Thatch.

The women oohed and aahed over each other's dresses. I wore an off the shoulder maxi dress embroidered with a garden's worth of flowers. The frock would have looked like ten million dollars with strappy sandals. I didn't care. My boots protected my feet and ankles from snake bites.

Liz wore white (a brave choice when barbeque was on the menu). The cotton dress had a square neckline and angel sleeves. Those flowing sleeves were another brave choice. Two words. Barbeque sauce.

Willa, who wore a seersucker shift, had caught her hair into a cool, elegant French twist. She leveled a stern gaze at the men in the group. "There will be no men at one end of the table, women at the other, tonight. Thatch and Perry, you sit with Ellison down there." She pointed. "Liz and I will sit with Anarchy."

We did as we were told.

A patchwork plaid cloth covered the picnic table and sweating mason jars filled with ice water waited at each setting. Fresh Queen Anne's lace and daisy made up the centerpieces.

I sat and reached for my water.

Perry took the seat to my left, and Thatch sat across from me.

"So." Thatch steepled his fingers. "The first thing we do, let's kill all the lawyers."

"Shakespeare?"

He nodded. "How goes the investigation?"

"You'd have to ask Anarchy," I replied.

"Yes, your husband, who's digging into our deepest, darkest secrets in hopes of discovering the killer."

"If you're innocent, you needn't worry."

He grinned as if I'd said something amusing. "Are you really that naïve?"

"Are you really that cynical?"

"Of the two of us, I am a lawyer."

"Of the two of us, I am the one who's been directly involved in a murder investigation."

"That's right. You were a suspect in Henry's murder."

"Proven innocent."

"It helps when you sleep with the detective." He glanced at the far end of the table. "Unfortunately, I don't think I'm Anarchy's type."

Anarchy and I hadn't so much as kissed for months after Henry's murder. Thatch's slimy insinuation couldn't be farther from the truth. "It also helped that I didn't kill Henry."

"Thatch Cooke," said Buffy. "You should be ashamed of yourself. You know Ellison's not a killer." She'd arrived while Thatch and I were sparring.

"Also, her husband is investigating you," Perry added. "You might try getting on her good side, rather than antagonizing her. She has the detective's ear."

Thatch shrugged. He wasn't worried. Either he was innocent or, if he was guilty, he didn't think Anarchy could prove he'd killed Graham.

At the moment, still smarting from his suggestion that I beat a murder rap by sleeping with Anarchy, I leaned toward the latter. "My husband is very good at his job."

Thatch's answering grin was almost feral.

"Where's Sumner?" Perry asked Buffy.

"She's resting in the clubhouse," she replied. "She didn't feel up to coming to dinner."

"Buffy, you sit down there," Willa called. "Bill come sit by me."

Bill? He stood behind Buffy, and I hadn't noticed him.

He followed Willa's instructions, and Buffy sat next to Thatch. "I take it we're talking about the murder?"

"What else?" said Perry.

Buffy opened her mouth as if she had an answer, but Misty and her staff appeared carrying platters of chicken wings with dipping sauce, crudité huddled around bowls of dill dip, and plates of tomatoes and mozzarella drizzled with balsamic and topped with basil.

"This looks marvelous," I told the caterer.

Misty offered me a tired smile. "I hope so. May I get anyone a drink?"

"More water for me, please." The wine had left me feeling muzzy.

Thatch and Perry requested bourbons. Buffy asked for a beer, and Mel, who joined our end of the table and sat next to me, wanted a gin and tonic.

"Ellison was just about to share her theories," Thatch told Mel. "Given her personal experience with murder, she's an expert."

"There's no need for sarcasm."

"Lighten up, Ellison. Can't you take a joke?" Which was

exactly what people said when they'd crossed a line and didn't want to be held accountable.

I forced a pleasant smile. "What are your theories, Thatch? Who killed Graham?"

Thatch glanced around the table, then grinned. "One of us."

Misty, who'd appeared with a pitcher, refilled my glass. Water splashed the tablecloth. Her hand shook as she put Buffy's beer on the table. Next she served Mel's gin and tonic, and finally, the men their bourbon. Then, she hurried away.

Thatch took a sip of his drink, then called to the other end of the table, "Jones, do you have a suspect?"

"Still plenty of options," Anarchy replied.

"Have you cleared anyone?"

The two men stared at each other, and Anarchy said, "Not yet."

Thatch laughed as Mel spluttered gin.

"What does he mean?" She scowled at me. "Fred and I have alibis."

"You're married," said Buffy.

"What's that supposed to mean?"

"Your alibi would be worth more if someone else saw you."

Mel twisted the napkin in her lap until it looked like a piece of rope. "It was barely dawn. We were asleep. Who else would see us?"

"Ellison saw Misty," said Buffy.

Mel snorted. "That's because Ellison has an unhealthy relationship with coffee."

Hey, now.

"Bill saw Misty," said Thatch. "Up early with the pretty caterer."

Buffy's face flushed a deep red.

Thatch was an ass. I glared at him. "Bill got coffee, then he went fishing."

Perry took in Buffy's complexion and said, "Ease up, Thatch." His voice was quiet but firm.

"Sorry, Buffy. I guess we're all a bit on edge." Thatch's unrepentant smirk belied his apology.

"We are," said Buffy. "On edge." She'd let him off the hook, but she looked as if she might cry.

"We're not used to murder like Ellison," said Perry.

I dug my elbow into his ribs. I would have jabbed him harder, but I sensed he was trying to distract Buffy.

"Oof!"

"Serves you right."

"How did your elbow get so pointy?" He rubbed his side. "Gain some weight woman."

"Liz," I called. "Your husband says the nicest things. I'm keeping him."

Anarchy raised his brows. "There's no room in the cabin."

"Sorry, Perry." I held up my hands in apology. "Anarchy says I can't keep you."

He grinned. "Story of my life."

"You're very disrespectful." Merit, who'd arrived late, wore a pinched expression.

"We need a break from sadness," I replied.

"No one at this table is sad." Merit made an excellent point. We were horrified or sickened or secretly glad. But no one grieved Graham.

"I should have said, we need a break from horror." Because murder was horrible.

She sniffed. "Is there anything here I can eat?"

"They haven't served dinner, but the vegetables look delicious." Buffy, who had chosen chicken wings, looked at my plate. "Ellison?"

"The caprese is marvelous."

Merit rolled her eyes. "I don't eat dairy."

The woman was beyond annoying. "Then have a carrot stick."

"Where's Tommy?" asked Buffy. "Is he joining us?"

"He's not feeling well."

"I'm sorry to hear that." And I meant it. Merit was easier to take when he was around.

"Hmph. Hopefully he'll feel better tomorrow."

Perry and Thatch exchanged a look, and I wondered what they knew.

"Sorry we're late!" Libba, who wore a backless halter dress in a barely-there gauzy material, took the seat next to Perry.

Charlie sat across from her and flashed a boyish grin. "We lost track of time."

I did not want or need additional details about what they'd been doing. But if I didn't come up with a topic fast, she'd tell us. I gathered my courage, and looked at Thatch. "Will you stay on as managing partner now that Graham is dead?"

"I didn't have any plans to step down when he was alive. Why would his death change anything?"

"I thought the managing partner job was a temporary post. A year or two, then the next lawyer took a turn."

"I'm exceptionally good at handling the firm's business."

"Graham didn't think so. He thought he could do better."

Thatch glared at me.

I glared back. I'd learned glaring at Mother's knee. Under her tutelage, I'd become a world-class glarer. And I could glare all night long.

Misty and her staff interrupted our glare-off, freeing me to look down the table at Anarchy.

He was deep in conversation with Willa, and I hoped he was learning something useful. Maybe something damning. I *wanted* Thatch to be guilty.

The servers filled the table with platters of barbeque, crocks of baked beans, a tray piled high with butter-slathered corn on the cob, and bowls of tossed salad. For a few blissful moments, talk of death and contested partnerships was put aside in favor of filling our plates.

I bit into a rib and moaned to Perry, "The caterer your wife hired is a genius."

Perry grinned. "Liz does everything well. I'd be lost without her."

Thatch laughed. Not a nice laugh.

Perry frowned across the table. "What?"

"Graham would never have nabbed your biggest client if it weren't for Liz." Thatch shifted his gaze my way. "She insisted they stay in Kansas City for your wedding reception. Graham went to North Carolina alone and came home as lead counsel."

That wasn't quite the story Liz had told.

"Graham got what was coming to him," said Buffy.

"Oh?" Thatch turned his attention to her. "How so?"

"He was a jerk."

Thatch tilted his head, and I got the sense that he was a hyena about to attack. "And that means his murder is justified?"

"We reap what we sow," said Merit. For once, her holier-than-thou attitude didn't bother me.

"Be that as it may," said Thatch. "It sounds as if Buffy is condoning murder. Some people just need killing?"

"Don't pretend you didn't want him dead," Buffy replied. "If the managing partner job had come up for a vote, you would have lost."

He shrugged. "I guess we'll never know."

"*Someone* had a reason to murder Graham."

Thatch pointed a pork rib at her. "People who live in glass houses..."

Buffy sat very straight and looked down her nose. "I'm sure I don't know what you mean."

"When Graham was doing due diligence for taking Bill's

company public, he found the corporate apartment on the Plaza. I believe a pretty young woman lived there."

"You're despicable."

Buffy wasn't wrong. She pushed away from the table. "I'm going to check on Sumner." Then, she strode toward the clubhouse.

Libba stared across the table. "Not cool, Thatcher. Not cool."

"She asked for it."

"She's a middle-aged mother of two. You're a highly paid attorney, who argues for a living. It wasn't a fair fight."

He rolled his eyes. I hated it when teen-aged girls did that. I especially hated it when grown men did it.

Libba gave him her best glare (not as good at Mother's or mine, but not bad). "David beat Goliath."

"What's that supposed to mean?"

"I got the sense that Buffy had ammunition she didn't use. Because, unlike you, she didn't want to throw a friend to the wolves." She jerked her thumb at me.

At me. I was the wolf in her scenario. Or, I was married to the wolf.

A dull red climbed Thatch's neck and touched his cheeks.

I silently cheered for Libba, even if she had called me a wolf.

"Has Anarchy heard back about the gun?" Mel pressed an open palm to her tanned chest.

"Not yet."

"How will I sleep tonight? The killer was in our cabin."

"The killer is at this table," said Thatch.

Mel gasped.

Merit fixed him with her pale gaze. "You enjoy making people feel uncomfortable. I wonder why that is. Does it give you an edge in arguments?"

"You've cut to the core of his lawyerly mystique." Perry turned to me. "I told you, there's a reason people hate lawyers."

"I'm beginning to see why."

"And you're not even looking at a bill."

"What will happen with Charlie's case?" asked Libba. "Now that Graham is dead."

Perry and Thatch exchanged a glance, and a nod, then Thatch said, "The firm won't touch it. In my estimation, it was a nuisance filing, designed to extort money from the hospital." He grimaced at Charlie. "That's not to say another lawyer won't pick it up, but we're out."

"Thanks, Thatch."

Just when I was ready to write him off, Thatch did something decent.

"Ellison, does Anarchy think we're safe?" Mel glanced around the table. "If there is a killer among us, he could strike again."

Perry saved me from responding. "Like everyone says, Graham was killed for a reason. Does anyone have a reason to want you dead?"

Mel shuddered. "Of course not."

"I wonder if that's true," said Merit.

Mel stiffened, but Merit didn't notice. "Maybe the killer has a taste for murder. Auden said, 'Evil is unspectacular and always human, and shares our bed and eats at our own table.'"

"You're quoting Auden at us?" Thatch scoffed.

"Evil is all around us, and because evil is everywhere, it's hard to contain. Maybe the killer likes killing. Or perhaps he discovered a taste for it when he shot Graham."

Despite the heat. I shivered.

"Merit, you're just a ball of sunshine," said Libba.

Merit turned her gaze on my friend. "We're taking about evil."

"We're talking about whoever killed a man none of us liked. We're wondering if it's likely the killer will act again. If you ask me, the answer is 'no.'"

I hoped she was right, but I lacked her certainty.

Libba wiped barbeque sauce from her fingers. "You'd better get used to talking about this weekend, because everyone and their brother will want a first-hand account."

"Gossip." Merit sniffed her disapproval.

Libba held up her freshly wiped hands and tilted her head. "I'm sure you'd rather talk about the nature of evil, but for most people the concept is too abstract. They know evil when they see it, or, in this case, hear about it secondhand."

Merit's expression was beyond sour.

"Wait a minute, Libba," said Thatch. "I think Merit may be onto something." Why was he encouraging her? "What is evil?"

"The taking of a human life," Mel replied.

Thatch frowned as if he wasn't entirely happy with her answer. "That's an evil act, but it doesn't encompass evil?"

"Evil is something profoundly immoral and wicked," said Merit.

Thatch tapped his lips with his index finger. "So cheating on my wife is wicked?"

"I think there's more to it," I said. "I think there needs to be an intent to harm. Cheating on your wife is definitely immoral, but it's not evil unless done with the intent to hurt her."

"I don't know, Ellison." Thatch's smile was all teeth. "Sounds like a gray area."

"I thought lawyers liked gray areas."

"We love gray areas," said Perry.

"So." Charlie draped an arm across Libba's bare shoulders. "Murder is immoral and wicked and includes intent to harm. It's evil."

"But does the killer see it that way?" I mused.

"What do you mean?" asked Libba.

"We're all the heroes of our own stories. Killers feel wronged or trapped. They may see taking a life as their only option."

Thatch smirked. "You speak from vast experience?"

"I've found a few bodies." So many I'd lost track.

"Murder is evil," said Mel. "Always. A killer knows what they're doing is wrong, and they do it anyway.

I wasn't about to argue the killer's side.

"No, no." Thatch wagged a pork rib. "Ellison makes a good point. No one wakes up and decides to be evil."

"What about people who plan murders down to the last detail?" said Merit.

Thatch frowned at her. "We're not in a Hitchcock movie or a Christie novel. Most murders are crimes of passion."

Merit curled her upper lip. "You mean a broken heart."

"I mean someone who's so angry, they act without thinking."

"Whoever killed Graham woke up this morning and decided to kill him," I said. "They had a night to sleep on their decision."

Thatch shook his head. "Maybe they didn't sleep. Maybe the stewed. They got more and more angry. They went to the cabin. They saw Sumner leave on her run. And they grabbed the opportunity to end Graham's life."

For a long second, I imagined the killer lurking in the woods. Waiting. And then common sense took over. "After they had the foresight to steal Perry's gun?"

"That's assuming Perry's gun was actually stolen." Thatch smirked at his law partner. "Did Graham do anything to tick you off last night?"

"No more so than usual."

"What do you think, Ellison. You're the one with all the experience." His tone was mocking. "Cold, calculated murder or crime of passion?"

"Does it have to be either or?"

Thatch folded his hands and rested them on the table's edge. "I believe it does."

"I don't. What if the killer had been thinking of killing Graham?" My gaze swept the table. "Nearly everyone had a reason to want him dead. They'd been thinking, but had no plans to actually commit murder. Then, something Graham did or said set them off. The killer was furious and already had a plan in place."

Thatch clapped slowly. "So, who among us is angry enough to kill?" He held my gaze and I felt like I was staring into the eyes of a snake.

"I don't know. But Anarchy will find them."

"Your faith is adorable."

"Anarchy has the best clear rate in the department."

"Domestic disputes. Drug deals gone wrong. Unneighborly neighbors. Solving those murders does not make him Hercule Poirot."

I tapped my napkin against my lips. "Being a suspect doesn't bother you?"

"Not in the least. Mark my words. This crime will never be solved."

Mel's breath caught. "We'll live under an umbrella of suspicion for the rest of our days?"

Thatch rolled his eyes. Again. "Don't be so dramatic, Mel. No one thinks you have the nerve to commit murder."

That Thatch—making friends left and right.

CHAPTER TEN

*a*narchy and I sat on the porch at the back of our cabin and night pressed against the screens. An owl hooted. An animal trotted past the edge of the clearing.

"Under different circumstances, I'd love this." He meant if I hadn't found a body.

We'd turned off the air-conditioner so we could have an actual conversation.

"It is beautiful out here." If one could get over the heat and the snakes and the murder.

He nodded. "How was dinner at your end of the table?"

"Just shy of litigious."

He chuckled. "You did get both lawyers."

"How about your end?"

"Willa and Liz are talkers."

"And?"

"When it comes to Graham, there's shock and horror, but not grief."

I nodded. "The only person I've seen show much emotion is Misty."

"Oh?"

"When I talked to her earlier today, she'd been crying."

Anarchy stared into darkness that seemed thicker and… darker than in the city.

"What are your theories?" I asked.

He reached across the small distance that separated us, and his fingers laced with mine. "You go first."

Or, we could forget about murder, go inside, and lose ourselves in each other.

"Ellison?"

"Right. Almost everyone has a motive. Almost no one has an alibi."

Anarchy held a glass of scotch in his free hand. He lifted the drink to his lips and took a sip. "So far, we're on the same page."

"Libba and Charlie are cleared."

"You're sure about that?"

"I am. If Libba were to commit murder, it would be to protect someone."

"Maybe she's protecting Charlie?"

"She wouldn't risk everything for a man—no matter how giddy she seems." I shook my head. "Besides, Thatch called the lawsuit a nuisance filing. Neither Libba nor Charlie would kill over that."

"What about Charlie's kids?"

"Charlie may not have been the best husband, but he adores his children. If there were an issue, he'd hire a tougher, meaner lawyer than his ex-wife. No way would he lose visitation rights."

"Noted."

"But you don't agree?"

"Time will tell."

"Moving on." I didn't want to debate Libba and Charlie with him. "I think Merit and Tommy are in the clear."

"Oh?"

"Merit, because she'd rather talk than act. And Tommy was too drunk."

"Drunks kill people."

"Not with one shot straight through the heart."

"You paid attention at the crime scene."

That sounded like praise, and not the you're-pretty kind (which was all well and good), but the you're-competent-and-smart-and-observant kind (which was so much better). Warmth bloomed in my chest, but I kept my tone nonchalant. "Not my first shooting. That leaves Liz and Perry, Willa and Thatch, Mel and Fred, Buffy and Bill, and Sumner."

"Add Misty."

"Oh?"

"When Randy left the clubhouse to feed the horses and muck their stalls, she wasn't in the kitchen."

We could add Misty. Her crying over a man she barely knew had seemed odd.

"For now, Perry and Liz. Perry has a motive. A good one. But I adore them both and don't want him to be guilty."

"That's not how this works. Sometimes nice people are guilty."

"I know," I huffed. "There's motive and opportunity. And the murder weapon probably belonged to him." I stared through the darkness at the man who held my hand. "When will we know for sure if his gun was used?"

"Monday. Motive, opportunity and the presumptive murder weapon. That should move them to the top of the list."

I tilted my head toward the ceiling fan. "I've known them forever. They're not killers. I'm sure of it. Does my gut count for anything?"

"This is your suspect list."

"Then it counts. They're not on my list. Next, there's Willa and Thatch. They also have motive and opportunity. Also, Thatch insisted that Sumner and Graham be invited this weekend. I don't understand that. Willa and Liz can talk about

Graham and Thatch and Perry being colleagues, but something seems off about inviting the Landinghams."

"Keep your enemies close?"

"Or set up a murder. Also, Thatch is a horse's ass. He said things at dinner…"

"What things?" Anarchy's voice was suddenly hard-edged. Had he heard Thatch's insinuations?

"He was cruel to Buffy." Somehow, I didn't want to repeat the things Thatch had suggested about me and Anarchy. "She left the table."

"What did Bill say?"

Bill had stared at his plate. The only hint of his feelings was the way he clutched his knife—as if he ached to plunge the blade into Thatch's chest. "Not much."

"What did he say, Ellison?"

"To Buffy?"

"To you. I saw you go pale."

"It doesn't matter." I meant that. Anarchy would think Thatch had besmirched my honor, and he'd have words with Thatch. Have words. Nope. I could fight my own battles. And this wasn't even a battle. Thatch's arrow had been so far off the mark, I could easily ignore the barb.

"To you. It doesn't matter to you. It matters to me."

"Please, let it go."

He huffed.

"I get the feeling Thatch is the spider at the center of an intricate web. Liz says there's a decent chance Graham would have replaced Thatch as managing partner. What if he's been embezzling from the firm? If Graham were elected, he'd have found the discrepancies."

"You really don't like him."

"I really don't."

"Your instincts are excellent. Next?"

"Mel and Fred. Graham may well have destroyed Fred's bank."

"Graham didn't make the loan. That was Fred's decision."

"True." I ceded. "But I'm not sure Fred or Mel would agree. Also, why did the gun turn up in their cabin? Did Fred do a bad job of hiding it?"

"Fred, not Mel?"

I thought back to finding the gun and the shock on Mel's face. "I can almost guarantee she had no idea the gun was in the couch. Also, at dinner, Mel seemed genuinely frightened by the prospect of a killer among us."

Anarchy rubbed his chin and sipped his scotch and stared into the night.

"I wonder if there's more to the bad loan? Did Graham somehow force Fred to make it?"

His gaze shifted to me. "You mean blackmail?"

"Yep. Graham was not a nice man. What's more, they don't have real alibis. Mel would lie for Fred in a heartbeat."

"So Fred's near the top of your list. What about Buffy and Bill?"

"Bill has an alibi."

Anarchy waggled his hand. "Not so much."

"But Misty saw him."

"He could have made it to the Landingham's cabin and shot Graham before you left for coffee. Also, Randy didn't see him on the dock."

"Interesting. Graham discovered Bill was using company funds to keep a mistress in an apartment on the Plaza. And Graham wasn't discreet. Thatch knew all about it."

"Is that what made Buffy leave the table?"

"Yes."

Anarchy rubbed his chin. "I wonder what else Graham found."

"Besides the apartment? I wondered that, too."

"So Bill has opportunity and motive. You only focused on the men. What about the wives?"

I shook my head. "Except for Sumner, I don't see it."

"Let's talk about Sumner."

I pictured Sumner as she'd been Friday night. She'd worn a low-cut dress, those spidery eyelashes, and a hopeful smile. She'd looked down the table often, smiling ever-brighter at Graham. "Unless there's life insurance, she's not getting a big payday."

"How do you know?"

"Women talk. Graham made a lot of money, but they spent it —that house." Far too big for two people. "They went on safari in Kenya this spring. Also, Sumner's jewelry. Did you notice the diamonds in her ears? At least a carat apiece." I scratched at a mosquito bite. "Actually, if there's life insurance, the firm may hold the policy. Graham was a rainmaker."

"Explain."

"Large law firms have partners and associates. There are levels of partnership, but let's keep this simple."

"Simple is good. Go on."

"Associates are paid a salary."

"Okay."

"Partners eat what they kill."

"Meaning?"

"They're paid for their billable hours, but the real money comes from bonuses. Bonuses are determined by the number of hours billed to a particular client or file. Oh!"

"What?"

"I thought Thatch was being decent when he said the firm would drop Dr. Adams' suit against Charlie."

"He wasn't?"

"Someone's always suing a hospital. As far as clients go, they're evergreen. New issues, new files each year. Thatch dropped the suit because he wants to stay on St. Mark's good side. The hospital is a potential client."

Anarchy rolled his shoulders. "So, when Graham stole Perry's client, he stole bonus money."

"Exactly. Think of a billable hour as a pie. From an associate's billable hours, the firm recoups the associate's salary and benefits. That's one portion. Another portion goes to over-head—lights, rent, support staff."

"I'm with you."

"Then there's the remainder. The firm puts what's left into a bonus pool. So, if Perry billed twenty to thirty hours a week to the file and had five associates billing twenty to thirty hours a week—"

"They split the bonus?"

And Thatch said I was naïve? "Nope. The associates get a small percentage, the firm gets a decent percentage, and lead counsel gets the lion's share."

"That could add up to a huge bonus."

"Yep. Back to the insurance. The firm keeps track of each partner's profitability. Windfalls, like life insurance pay-outs, are divvied up based on each partner's contributions to the firm's bottom line."

"And Thatch determines that?"

"Yes and no. But, here's the kicker. Since Thatch is managing partner, he gets to claim managerial hours rather than billable hours to determine his bonus."

"So, he might get a hefty chunk of any insurance policy taken out on Graham?"

"If the firm had a policy? Definitely." I brushed a stray hair away from my face. "Actually, Sumner and the firm could both have policies."

"I'll find out." Anarchy finished his scotch and put the glass on an end table. "Let's return to Sumner."

"We only have her word that Graham was alive when she went running."

He exhaled a frustrated sigh. "That blasted air-conditioner. Without the noise, I would have heard the gunshot. Assuming Sumner is guilty, and she didn't kill for the money, what other motive could she have?"

"Graham had an affair."

He sat a bit straighter. "Oh?"

"Buffy said it was someone at the firm."

"Who's her source?"

"I assume Sumner. Buffy told me the affair ended, and Sumner and Graham went to marital counseling."

He tapped a knuckle against his teeth. "I'm not seeing a motive."

"Neither am I."

"What about Misty?"

I gave the idea brief consideration. "The law firm is her best client. I doubt she'd start killing the partners."

"So, you're picking Thatch, Fred or Bill?"

I nodded. "In that order. What about you? Who's your top suspect?"

"You're not going to like it."

"Who?"

"Perry."

∽

Anarchy slept next to me.

I'd counted sheep, practiced deep breathing, and tried progressive relaxation. Nothing worked. And Anarchy's ability to tumble into slumber and stay there was beginning to annoy me.

I fumbled for my watch on the bedside table. Four in the morning. I'd been awake since three. Experience told me if I hadn't yet managed to fall asleep after an hour, it wasn't happening. My best course of action was to read or sketch for an hour before I tried again.

I slipped out of bed, grabbed my sketchbook, and headed to the screen porch.

The darkness was near absolute, and I took a minute to listen to the night's sounds. An owl hooted. The same one as before? Leaves rustled. A bird shrieked, and I pitied the small animal clasped in its talons. A breeze tickled my bare arms. Insects and birds and small animals made tiny noises that seemed large in the darkness.

If I turned on the light to sketch, I'd be spotlighted. Anything out there could see me, and I'd be blind.

I put my sketchbook on the table and sank into a chair, brought my knees to my chin, and wrapped my arms around my shins.

What a mess this weekend had turned out to be.

Graham was dead.

The heat was almost unbearable.

People who'd been friends for years were turning on each other.

And some of my favorite people were murder suspects.

Also, I missed Grace. I missed Aggie. I missed Max. I missed an air-conditioner that didn't sound like a diesel truck without a muffler. I missed Mr. Coffee.

I let my feet fall to the floor and straightened my shoulders. Anarchy would catch the killer and we'd leave. Soon. Hopefully, we'd make it home in time for Sunday dinner.

A crash in the woods stilled the night sounds. Whatever was crashing about came from the direction of Sumner's cabin. And it was big. A wild hog? Those things were dangerous. A second crash brought me to my feet.

I listened. Hard. And heard sobbing.

Sobbing?

"Who's out there?"

"Ellison?" More of a croak than a voice. "Help."

I rushed into the house, jammed my feet in boots, and poked Anarchy awake. "There's someone out there."

He blinked and groaned. "What? What time is it?"

"Outside. There's someone. They need help."

He pulled a pillow over his head. "You had a dream, sweetheart."

"No. I was on the screen porch. I heard someone. They said my name and 'help.'"

Anarchy sat up. "You're sure?"

"Positive."

He got out of bed, pulled on a pair of shorts, and collected his gun.

"You think we'll need that?"

"Someone was murdered last night." He made an excellent point. "We also need a flashlight."

"There's one in the drawer by the sink." I found it and turned toward him. "You can't go barefoot."

He put on the Chuck Taylors I hadn't thrown away, and, together, we stepped onto the front porch and into the night.

"Hello," I whisper-called.

No one answered.

Anarchy ran his fingers through his sleep-tussled hair. "You're sure you heard someone?"

"They were coming from that direction." I pointed toward Sumner's cabin. Then I stepped off the porch.

"Ellison, wait."

"Someone needs our help."

"You've got the only flashlight."

"Oh, right. Sorry. Are you coming?"

We walked half-way to Sumner's cabin, and Anarchy said, "Point the light downward."

I did as he asked and saw a black puddle. Black. But the darkness washed away color. I gulped. "Is that blood?"

He bent, touched the wetness with his index finger, then smelled his hand. "Looks that way. What exactly did you hear?"

"A shriek. I thought it was a bird. Then I thought an animal was crashing through the brush. Then I heard my name."

I couldn't see his expression in the dark, but I'm fairly certain he frowned. "Maybe you should go back to the cabin."

"And leave you alone out here? Not on your life."

"You were on the porch?

"I was. Whoever called my name must have been in the woods." I swept the flashlight's beam toward the trees to our left.

"Hold up."

I kept the beam steady as Anarchy studied a bush with a broken branch.

"This way."

"Into the woods?" I squeaked.

"Give me the flashlight and I'll go alone."

I tamped down my fears (did snakes sleep at night?) and joined him.

A mosquito found me, then he told all his buddies about the all-you-can-eat buffet. The flashlight beam jerked as I batted away insects. Branches snagged my nightgown and scratched at my skin. I was in hell. There was only one thing that could make this trek through the woods worse.

"Anarchy?"

"Yes?"

"Do snakes sleep at night?" I held my breath, waiting for his answer.

"They're cold-blooded creatures. They're active in the daytime."

Air escaped my lungs in a giant whoosh. "You're sure?"

"You're wearing boots."

"But are they high enough?" I pushed aside a branch that had tried to take out my right eye. "And you're wearing sneakers."

An owl hooted, and I shivered.

"We'll be fine." He walked slowly, occasionally stopping to exam a branch or ask me to point the beam left or right.

"There." He pointed.

Fifteen feet away, the flashlight's beam found a woman's hand.

I stepped closer, and the beam illuminated the lower half of her body.

"Oh, no." My stomach did a barrel roll. "It's Buffy."

"How can you tell?"

"She's wearing cowboy boots with her nightgown."

Anarchy closed the distance to the body, fell to his knees, and searched for a pulse.

"Is she?" I already knew. No way, no how, would a living, breathing Buffy be on the forest floor when there were snakes around.

"She's gone." He held out his hand for the flashlight, and I gave it to him.

In Anarchy's hands, the beam played across her body. Its light caught the handle of a knife protruding from her stomach, and Anarchy swore softly.

I covered my mouth with my hands and closed my eyes.

When I opened them, Anarchy had moved the flashlight's beam to her face, which was covered by her hair.

He reached, as if he meant to move the strands, and I heard it.

Hssss.

"Anarchy, don't—"

My warning came too late. A snake sank its fangs deep into his wrist.

CHAPTER ELEVEN

*D*arkness danced at the edge of my vision, and I clutched the trunk of the nearest tree.

"Ellison."

My knees shook like Jell-O, and the only thing keeping me upright was my fear of what might be slithering across the forest floor.

"Ellison."

I was barely a bride and soon I'd be a widow. A sob rose from my belly and I pressed my hand to my mouth.

"Ellison!"

"I love you." Tears ran unchecked down my cheeks.

"I love you, too." He sounded annoyed. Why was Anarchy annoyed?

"These last few months with you have been the happiest of my life."

"I'm not going to die."

"You're not?" Did I dare hope?

"I'm not dying. But I need your help. Go find Randy. Tell him we need the sheriff and an ambulance."

I tore my gaze away from Anarchy and glanced at Buffy. "She's dead."

"The ambulance is for me."

"Right."

"The faster you find Randy, the faster help will arrive, the faster a doctor can administer anti-venom."

"What are you going to do?"

"Sit here and keep my heart rate down."

I stared at him. Was he crazy? It was dark. There was a body. There were snakes.

"Sweetheart, you're in shock, but we need help. Can you get Randy?"

"Get Randy?"

"Don't 'get' him. We don't need him here. Have him call for help."

"I can do that." If I could remember how to walk.

"Ellison."

"I'm going."

"Wait."

He was going to tell me he loved me one last time. A romantic declaration I'd remember until the end of my days. And I'd reply with…I had nothing. Nothing but an aching chasm where my heart should be.

"Ellison!"

I focused on my husband. We might only have a few minutes left.

"Here. Take the flashlight."

The flashlight? "I'm not leaving you alone in the dark."

"You need the light to find the path. To get help."

"Right." I took the flashlight from his outstretched hand. What if I never saw him again? Never heard the way he said my name? "You promise not to die?"

"I promise."

"I'll hold you to that."

"Ellison."

"What?"

"Be careful. Whoever killed Buffy could be out there."

And he wanted me to leave him alone in the dark?

"Go," he told me. "Hurry."

I turned and ran and didn't stop until I reached the path. There, I paused, ripped a strip of fabric from the bottom of my nightgown, and tied it to a tree.

Then I ran again. The path was ten times longer than it was during daylight hours. My breath came in short, hard pants. And a stitch in my side threatened to bring me to my knees.

Finally, I reached the clubhouse and pounded on the door. "Randy!"

He didn't answer.

I pounded harder.

The door jerked open, and the man on the other side gaped at me. "Mrs. Jones, what's wrong?"

"It's Anarchy. He was bitten by a snake. We need the police and an ambulance."

He peered past me. "Where is he?"

"The woods."

Randy, who wore plaid pajamas, frowned. "Why is he in the woods?"

"Snake. Bite. He could be dying. Please, call the ambulance and the police."

"We don't need the police for a snake bite."

"The police are for the body."

"The body?"

"There's been another murder."

He held up his hands. "Hold on. What happened to you?" His gaze took in my scratched skin, ripped nightgown, tear-stained cheeks, tangled hair, and cowboy boots.

"I heard someone in the woods. Anarchy and I went to investigate. We found a body—Buffy Geller's body. Then a snake bit Anarchy." That last part was the most important. "He needs an ambulance."

"You found a body yesterday."

"I'm aware. This is a new body. Would you please call an ambulance?" When he continued to stand there with his mouth hanging open, I asked, "Or let me use the phone?"

He opened the door wider. "Come in. I'll call."

I followed him to his office, where he called emergency services and explained our two problems. He hung up and turned to me. "They're on their way. Why didn't the detective come with you?"

"Snake bite. Let's go."

"Where?"

"The woods. Anarchy is still in the woods." Alone. Possibly dying.

Randy was slow on the uptake.

"If we go to him now, the emergency personnel won't know where to find him." He made a good point. Right now, waiting for men who could get Anarchy to a hospital was more important than my need to be with him.

"How long until the ambulance gets here?"

"Twenty minutes." He rubbed his palm across his mouth. "Would you like to borrow a shirt?"

I glanced down at my sheer nightgown and blushed. "That would be nice."

He brought me a clean denim shirt, and I put it on and rolled up the sleeves. The shirt's hem only reached my upper thighs. I didn't complain. The length was still lower than the remnants of my nightgown.

"Band-aids? Antiseptic cream?"

"My husband's alone in the woods. Snake venom is running through his veins. I'll worry about my cuts and bruises later."

He took a step back. "I could make coffee."

"Please."

Ten minutes later, I was sipping from a Styrofoam cup, watching the drive for signs of an emergency vehicle. Bear had hauled himself off the floor, and leaned against my leg in the doggy version of a hug.

Randy, who'd changed into jeans, a plaid shirt, and cowboy boots, joined me at the window. "May I get you anything else?" I kept my gaze locked on the drive. "No, thank—they're here." I ran outside, up the short path to the lot, and prayed the vehicle I'd spotted was the ambulance.

A patrol car pulled into the parking lot, and I swallowed my disappointment.

I sighed and glanced at Randy, who'd followed me. "I'll show them where the body is. Will you follow with the EMTs?"

"How do I find you?"

"I tore off part of my nightgown to mark where I came out of the woods. It's on the path between our cabin and Sumner's."

"We'll come as soon as they arrive."

"Thank you." I left him and approached the sheriff's deputy in the parking lot.

"I'm Deputy Kincaid." He looked at my boots and my shirt and my hair and frowned. He found me less than impressive. "Are you Mrs. Jones?"

"I am." And I wasn't impressed with him either. He was the kind of man whose 32-inch belt hovered well below his 44-inch waist. But, he was my only option. "If you'll come with me?"

"Hold up there, ma'am. Tell me what happened."

"I heard something in the woods. My husband and I went to investigate, and we found a body. Then a snake bit my husband."

He held up his pointer finger and wagged from side to side. "You found a body? A human body?"

"Yes. Didn't Randy tell you? I can take you to it."

"If you don't mind my saying, you seem real calm for a woman who found a body."

Was he kidding? "This isn't my first rodeo."

"Pardon?"

"My husband is a homicide detective. Ask Deputy Harden. He'll vouch for me."

"You're the woman who found the body yesterday?"

"Yes."

"Ma'am, you're plum unlucky."

I gritted my teeth. "Yes. I know."

I saw lights out the corner of my eye. "The ambulance is here!"

"Thought you said it was a dead body."

"My husband was bitten by a snake." Didn't he listen?

I left the deputy and hurried to the fit, young men exiting the ambulance. "My husband—"

"Snake bite?"

"That's right."

"Where is he, ma'am?"

"In the woods."

The two men exchanged a worried glance. "Can you find him?"

"Yes. Follow me. We'll have to walk. There's no road." If Deputy Kincaid wanted to come, he could. Or not. Either way, I wasn't wasting any more time on his questions.

I trotted past seven cabins, then slowed and searched the trees. "There." A strip of delicate silk fluttered in the light breeze. "Anarchy?"

"Here."

"Your husband's name is Anarchy?" asked the deputy.

"His parents were hippies before it was cool."

We tromped through the woods, following the sound of Anarchy's voice.

The EMTs stopped short when they saw Buffy. "What happened?"

"We found her." Not to be cold, but she was beyond their help. They needed to focus on Anarchy. "My husband needs you."

The older EMT nodded. "What kind of snake?"

"A copperhead," Anarchy replied.

I swayed.

"They're not deadly, Ellison."

"But they can make you very sick. We need to get you to a hospital, sir."

"I need a statement first," said the deputy.

I had a statement—Deputy Kincaid was an idiot. I bit my tongue and counted to ten. "I'll give the statement. Take Anarchy to the hospital. Please."

Dawn broke as I sat in the clubhouse with Randy and Deputy Kincaid

On the plus side, I'd stopped by the cabin, showered, and put on clothes. Bear was glued to my side, and he didn't have gas (a huge plus). Also on the plus side, coffee. Lots of coffee.

On the minus side, Buffy was dead. Anarchy was in the hospital. I had to deal with a sheriff's deputy who'd had his feelings hurt when the crime scene people kicked him off their scene. And somehow, he'd decided that expulsion was my fault.

When the deputy got up to refill his coffee, I whispered to Randy, "For the love of Pete, call Deputy Harden."

He nodded and disappeared into his office.

Bear watched him go, but stayed with me.

I scratched behind his ears.

Deputy Kincaid resumed his seat and crossed his ankle over his knee. "Let's go through this again."

I'd been trained to be polite to people in authority, and it was only that training that kept me from snapping at the man. "I couldn't sleep, so I stepped out onto the screen porch. I heard someone call my name and ask for help. I woke up my husband. Together, we went into the woods and found Buffy."

"You found Mr. Landingham's body as well?"

"Yes."

"Are you familiar with the expression, 'where there's smoke, there's fire?'"

"What are you suggesting, Deputy Kincaid?"

"It's quite a coincidence, you finding two bodies in two days."

Had I ever found two bodies on the same day? I couldn't remember. "You do realize my husband is a homicide detective?"

He leaned back in his chair and sipped his coffee. "You told me."

"He's working with your sheriff to solve Graham's murder. Call him. Ask him."

"Nobody calls the sheriff before seven."

"In the meantime, Bill Geller may wake up and wonder where his wife is." Heck, Bill might be on the run. He'd had a motive to kill Graham, and now Buffy was dead, too.

"We don't have murders down here. Worst that happens is hunting accidents. You people arrive, and we got two."

Randy stepped back into the room and gave a tiny nod.

I glanced at my watch. Six. "I'm going to call the hospital."

"We're not done," said Deputy Kincaid.

"For now, we are." I escaped into Randy's office, where he'd left the hospital's phone number on the desk for me.

I dialed and asked for Detective Jones' room.

"It's too early for calls, ma'am."

"This is his wife."

"Yes, ma'am. It's still too early."

My jaw clenched. "He was admitted in the past hour. With a snake bite."

"It's too early for calls."

"May I speak with his doctor?"

"The doctor is on rounds."

"So, if I can't speak to my husband and I can't speak to his doctor, with whom can I speak?"

"You're speaking with me."

"Your name, please." I sounded like Mother.

"Florence."

"Florence, can you update me on my husband's condition?"

"No, ma'am."

"Can you connect me with someone who can?"

"No, ma'am."

"Why not?"

"It's too early for calls."

I stifled a scream. "May I leave a message?"

"I'll take it down."

I had no faith she'd actually give the message to Anarchy, but I gave her the number.

"Spell the last name, please."

"J.O.N.E.S." She was messing with me. It was time to call in the big guns. "Thank you, Florence." For nothing, Florence. I hung up and dialed a different number.

"Hello." The voice was sleepy and surprised, but still held authority.

"Mother, it's Ellison. I need your help." I explained to her what had happened.

"Buffy Geller is dead, and you found the body?"

"You're missing the important part of the story."

"Not the part that's important to the Gellers."

I hated when she was right. "Yes," I admitted. "That's important to the Gellers. But Anarchy was bitten by a snake—a copperhead. He was taken to the Miami County Hospital, and no one there will tell me how he is. They won't connect me to his room. Nothing. "

"Why don't you go to the hospital?"

"I can't."

"Why not?"

"There's a sheriff's deputy questioning me."

"You're a suspect?" She sounded suitably outraged.

"Yes. And when he's done. Someone needs to tell Bill about Buffy. Deputy Kicked-in-the-Head will make a mess of it."

"Kicked-in-the-Head?"

"His real name is Kincaid, but Kicked-in-the-Head is so apt."

"What do you need from me?"

"Find out how Anarchy is. Please."

"Consider it done. Where should I call?"

I gave her both the hospital and club's numbers. "If you call here, Randy may answer the phone. Be nice. He's one of the good ones."

"I'm always nice." We both knew that was a big, fat lie.

"Thank you. I appreciate this." More than I could say.

"You're welcome, dear."

I returned to the deputy, who smirked at me. "How did your call with the hospital go?"

Had he asked Florence to snow me? I narrowed my eyes. "Not well. I called Kansas City."

His grin widened.

"I have someone calling the governor."

He glanced at his watch. "The governor's office is closed."

"They're not calling his office. They have his home number. And if Governor Docking can't help, they'll call Senator Dole." I resumed my seat. "Now, would you like to continue insinuating I had a part in a murder?"

After the night I'd had, watching Deputy Kicked-in-the-Head's complexion go from a healthy tan to a shade whiter than skim milk was very satisfying.

"Mrs. Jones?" Deputy Harden strode into the room.

Thank heavens. I rose, and Bear's tail thumped the floor. "Deputy."

"What happened?"

I recounted the story for the hundredth time.

"How's Detective Jones?" Finally, someone who understood the important part.

I glanced at Deputy Kicked-in-the-Head. "The hospital wasn't forthcoming."

Deputy Harden frowned.

"My mother is calling."

"Your mother?"

"It's best not to cross her." Deputy Kicked-in-the-Head and Florence were in for a world of trouble.

"Has anyone talked to Mr. Geller?" he asked.

I nodded toward Deputy Kicked-in-the-Head. "No. Deputy Kincaid has been exploring my possible guilt in the murders."

Deputy Harden exhaled. Slowly. "Would you speak to Mr. Geller with me? Please?"

"Yes."

Together, we walked to Bill's cabin. Bear, who seemed unwilling to let me out of his sight, tagged along.

"How would you like to handle this?" he asked.

He was asking me? "Isn't there a procedure?"

"We don't get a lot of murders down here."

"We tell Bill and gauge his reaction?"

The deputy nodded and rapped on the cabin door.

"Coming." A moment later, Bill answered. He wore rumpled pajamas and smelled of cigarettes and coffee. Purple half-moons hung beneath his eyes.

"Bill, this is Deputy Harden. He—"

"We met yesterday. What is this about?"

"It's about Buffy. She—"

"You've arrested her." He sagged against the door frame. "I knew something was wrong when I saw her empty bed."

"You think Buffy killed Graham?"

He frowned. "Don't you?"

Not until now. "Why do you think that?"

He peered past us, as if he was worried about eavesdroppers. "Come in."

Inside the cabin, a lit cigarette perched on the edge of an ashtray. Outside, the air was fresh and clean and not yet unbearably hot. "How about if we talk on the front porch?"

Bill considered, then nodded. "Give me a minute."

I watched through the screen as he pulled a seersucker robe over his pajamas and stubbed out his cigarette. Then, he joined us outside.

"Why do you think Buffy's been arrested?"

Bill rubbed the back of his neck, adjusted the robe's tie at his waist, and cracked. "She's not here. And she lied."

I lifted my brows. "About what?"

"She wasn't here in the cabin yesterday morning when Graham was killed. I came back here after I got coffee, and she was gone."

"You think Buffy was involved in Graham's death?"

"Why else would she lie?"

"Did you ask her where she was?"

"She said she followed me." His cheeks flushed. "She thought I might try my luck with the caterer."

"Did you?"

"I cast a lure, but the fish wasn't biting." He sounded vaguely surprised.

Imagine that, a successful, smart, young woman had passed on a middle-aged, married man. "Buffy didn't follow you back to the cabin?"

"If she did, I never saw her."

Had she seen the killer? I tried to remember every word of every conversation I'd had with Buffy yesterday. Had she dropped a hint?

"Did your husband arrest her?" Bill patted the pocket of his robe as if looking for a pack of cigarettes, then swore softy.

I didn't want to do this. Not at all. "No, Buffy hasn't been arrested."

"Then, where is she?" He sounded annoyed.

I swallowed a lump in my throat. "Buffy was murdered."

He stared at me. "That's not funny, Ellison."

It really wasn't.

"She was stabbed."

He stared for another few seconds, then shook his head and sank onto one of the two chairs on the front porch. "That can't be right."

"I'm sorry."

Bill looked up and searched my face. When he failed to find a shred of hope, his shoulders sagged, and his fingers laced together to make one fist that he pressed against his sternum. "You're sure?"

I wished I wasn't. "I'm sorry." The words weren't nearly enough.

Tears swam in his eyes. "How? Where?"

"Anarchy and I found her in the woods."

"The woods? Buffy? Where is she now? I want to see her."

Next to me, Deputy Harden cleared his throat. "Her body's being transported to the county medical examiner's office."

"To the morgue." Bill's voice broke on the word morgue.

"Yes, sir. I'm sorry for your loss."

Bill stared sightlessly at the path running by the cabin and rocked in his upright chair. His face was a study in devastation.

I couldn't clear the man in Graham's death, but I'd bet a million dollars Bill was innocent of his wife's murder.

Long, uncomfortable minutes passed. Bill rocked. Deputy Harden tugged at the collar of his uniform. Bear pressed against my left leg. And I wondered who else Buffy saw when she'd followed her husband.

Finally, Bill asked, "Is Anarchy investigating?"

"He will." I prayed he would.

"What's he doing, now? Why isn't he here?" He scowled at me, as if I were responsible for Anarchy's absence. "What could be more important than finding Buffy's killer?"

"Mrs. Jones!" Randy's call came from the path, halfway to the clubhouse. "The hospital is on the phone. They say it's urgent."

I took off at a run with Bear at my heels.

CHAPTER TWELVE

*T*he telephone was nestled amongst the magazines and ledgers on Randy's desk. I snatched the receiver and pressed it against my ear. "Hello."

"Mrs. Jones?" The voice was unfamiliar.

"This is she."

"This is Dr. Collins. I'm chief of staff at Miami County Hospital."

I couldn't breathe. I barely managed a whisper. "Yes?"

"You called earlier about your husband." Deep regret suffused his voice.

I sank into Randy's desk chair. The doctor was calling with awful news. They'd messed up the anti-venom, and Anarchy was dead. I should have insisted the ambulance take him to a trauma center in Kansas City. This was my fault. I clutched the edge of the desk with my free hand. "What has happened?"

Bear rested his graying chin on my leg and stared at me with liquid eyes.

"I understand our receptionist refused to put through your call."

I'd missed my chance to say goodbye. I closed my eyes. I couldn't look at a world without Anarchy in it.

"I'm sorry—"

A keening sob rose from my chest and broke free.

Bear whined in sympathy.

"I didn't realize it was that upsetting." He sounded positively horrified at my display of emotion.

"My husband is dead." If Dr. Collins didn't think that would be upsetting, there was something seriously wrong with him.

"What? No, he's not. I'm apologizing for our receptionist."

He was apologizing for Florence? The regret I heard in his voice was Mother-induced? Not because they'd botched Anarchy's care? "How's my husband?" I held my breath as I waited for his answer.

"He's under observation in the ICU."

"Intensive Care?"

"So we can keep a close eye on him. We see hundreds of snake bites a year and haven't lost a patient yet. He'll be fine. Good as new. I promise." He was trying to comfort me? Too little, too late. In fact, I wanted to introduce Dr. Collins to a nest of copperheads.

"May I speak with him, please?"

"Of course, I'll connect you." He cleared his throat. "I hope you're not too upset about the earlier mix-up."

That nest of copperheads still seemed like a good option. Or I could ask Mother to call again. The thought brought an evil smile to my lips. "Take good care of my husband, and I'll forget all about it."

I waited through thirty long seconds of dreadful hold music, then Anarchy said, "Hello."

Relief flooded my veins. "It's me. How are you?"

"In the future, when someone yells 'snake,' I'll be on the dinner table with you."

"That bad?"

"It's no picnic, but the doctors say I'll be fine. What's happening there?"

"Deputy Harden and I talked to Bill."

"Those conversations are never easy."

"It was awful. Because he cheated on her, I didn't realize Bill had feelings for Buffy. He loved her, at least in his own way, and I don't think he killed her."

Bear nudged me, and I scratched behind his ears.

"Also, Buffy lied about her whereabouts yesterday morning. She wasn't asleep. She followed Bill."

"Why?"

"Why did she follow him or why did she lie?"

"Start with follow."

"Good. I have an answer for that one. She suspected Bill had planned a rendez-vous with Misty."

"Had he?"

"Nope. No rendez-vous. He tried to pick her up. She shot him down. As to why Buffy lied…"

"Buffy saw the killer." Anarchy reached that conclusion much faster than I had.

"It sure seems that way."

"What's Harden doing now?"

"I left him with Bill." No need to tell Anarchy about my mad dash to the phone.

"Have him question everyone."

"I will. Although, they'll say they were sleeping." I switched to Bear's other ear. "You're sure you're okay?"

He chuckled. "You're not getting rid of me this easily."

"I'm counting on at least fifty years with you."

"I'll hold you to that."

A goofy smile touched my lips. "I don't know how far away the hospital is, but I'll be there as soon as I can."

He cleared his throat. "Would you do something for me?"

"Anything."

"Don't come."

The smile disappeared. "What? Why not?"

"Stay there. Catalog your impressions, your observations. You notice things."

"But—"

"Please?"

He was alone in a po-dunk hospital run by an idiot. He needed me. "Everyone is supposed to be leaving after brunch."

"That was before Buffy died. The sheriff will want to talk to them. Please. Stay. You're our best chance of solving these murders."

I wanted to see him with my own eyes. "You're not hiding anything? You're truly okay?"

"Truly."

"I love you." Almost losing him had reminded me how much.

"I love you, too. Stay at the club. Observe. Ask questions if you must. And *be careful*. Two people are dead, and I'm not there to protect you."

"I'll do it. I'll stay. But the moment everyone heads back to Kansas City, I'm coming."

"Fair enough."

"You sound tired. You should rest."

"I love you, Ellison. So much. I'll see you soon." He hung up.

I replaced the receiver and considered calling Mother. I owed her a debt of gratitude. But little-to-no sleep and two massive adrenalin jolts had left me feeling jittery and weak. And that was no condition for dealing with Mother. Then there was the shaking in my hands, which had nothing—absolutely nothing—to do with the amount of coffee I'd guzzled while waiting for the police and talking to Deputy Kicked-in-the-Head.

Something solid in my stomach wouldn't be amiss.

I'd call Mother when I felt better.

Bear and I headed to the kitchen, where Misty was taking a

sheet pan from the oven. She looked at the dog, raised a brow, but withheld comment.

"Whatever that is, it smells divine."

"Thank you. I made biscuits. Would you like one? I have honey butter and homemade strawberry jam."

"Yes, please."

She nodded at a long pine table surrounded by mismatched chairs. "Coffee?"

"Tempting, but I might have heart palpitations if I drink more caffeine." I sat at the table and breathed the heavenly aroma of Misty's baked goods.

Bear dropped on the floor next to me.

"A glass of water?" she asked.

"That would be lovely."

She poured my drink, put it on the table in front of me, then glanced out the window at the parking lot. "Two deputies, today."

"One for each murder."

She stiffened. "Two murders?"

"I'm sorry. I thought you knew." Deputy Kicked-in-the-Head had been in and out of the clubhouse, and he was neither quiet nor discreet.

"I didn't know. Who?"

"Buffy Geller."

She pulled out a chair from the table. "Do you mind if I sit? What happened?"

"My husband and I found her this morning. She'd been stabbed."

Misty gasped and pressed her fingers to her suddenly pale cheeks.

"Is something wrong?"

She glanced at the counter, then her worried gaze found mine. "One of my knives is missing."

That wasn't good. "When did you notice it was gone?"

"When I came in this morning."

I glanced at the tray of cooling biscuits. "You came in and checked your knives?"

"I chopped peppers and mushrooms for a strata."

"Is anything else missing?"

"Not that I can tell." She stared at the table's scarred surface. "Randy keeps the place locked at night. There's a display of antique shotguns that are apparently quite valuable. But, when I arrived this morning, the back door was unlocked."

I made a mental note to ask Randy about that. "Do you normally leave your knives in the kitchen overnight?" Aggie's beau, Mac, was also a professional chef, and he was a bit obsessive about his knives.

"I figured they were safe, and I don't need them at the lodge."

"Are they a set?"

"Yes." That meant the handles to each blade would look alike.

"You're sure the missing knife was with the others last night?"

"Positive." She gulped. "You don't think the killer used my knife?"

A missing knife and a stabbed woman. Two plus two usually made four. "May I see one of your other knives?"

She fetched her case from the counter and withdrew a paring knife.

I ignored the blade and studied the handle. I'd been so unnerved by the trek through the dark woods, finding Buffy's body, and the snake bite, that I'd forgotten what the knife looked like. I couldn't describe the murder weapon if my life depended on it.

"Is it the same?" She caught her lower lip in her teeth and reclaimed her seat.

"I honestly can't tell. Which knife is missing?"

She rested one hand on her tummy and the other on the table. "My utility knife. What if it was used in a murder?"

"How long is the blade?"

"Six inches."

Two plus two equaled four.

"I'll ask Deputy Harden to bring by a picture of the knife. He can compare the handles."

She stood abruptly and returned to the counter where the biscuits cooled. "I meant to get you a biscuit."

"Even if the killer used your knife, Buffy's murder isn't your fault."

Her shoulders hunched.

"Have you noticed anything this weekend?" I asked. "Things that seem...strange?"

She put a plate with two warm, golden biscuits in front of me, then added a crock of butter and a jam jar.

"Thank you."

"You're welcome. You live in a strange world, Mrs. Jones."

I sliced open a biscuit. "What do you mean?"

"You're all friends, but you don't really like each other."

"Yes, and no. There are women here who've been my friends since I was a toddler. They'll be my friends for the rest of my life." Libba and I were together for the long haul.

"The rest?"

"You're right about the rest. Friends of circumstance rather than the heart."

"What was Mrs. Geller?"

"To me? We were friendly. We knew the same people, as did our mothers before us. We might meet for lunch or invite each other to cocktail parties, but we weren't close. Nor was she close with Libba or Liz. I can't speak to her relationships with the other women."

"What about Mrs. Landingham?"

"I don't know her very well." She definitely fell in the friends of circumstance category. "Why do you ask?"

Misty wiped her clean, dry hands on a towel. "It must be

awful, losing her husband like that." She turned back to the oven and fiddled with the knobs. "Were they happy?"

"Honestly, I don't know. I know he had an affair."

Misty looked over her shoulder. "I—"

"There you are." Randy burst into the kitchen. "How's your husband?"

"Doing fine."

Bear's tail thwacked the floor, and he grinned.

"What a relief. I wanted to stay with you, but the horses needed to be fed and turned out. Then Jepp found me and wanted to know what's happening. We've never had a weekend like this one."

"You've been very kind." I glanced at Misty, who had her back to us. "We have a little mystery."

Randy crouched on the floor and rubbed Bear's face. "Oh?"

"When Misty arrived this morning, the back door was unlocked."

Randy stopped rubbing and frowned. "I locked it before I went to bed. I made sure, what with a gun thief running around."

"And a killer," Misty added.

Randy stood, went to the back door, examined the lock from both sides, then scratched his head. "Maybe I forgot. I've had a lot on my mind."

The poor man. First Graham's murder And now, Buffy's. I pushed my plate toward him. "Try a biscuit. They're delicious."

"You're sure?"

"You're saving my waistline."

"Don't mind if I do." He took a bite and grinned at Misty. "You're welcome here anytime. Heck, don't leave. Stay."

She flushed.

"I mean it," Randy continued. "The diner in town is for sale. You'd make a huge success of it."

Misty ducked her head.

"And, you could cater large events here at the club. Think about it. Small town. Slower pace. A great place to raise a family." His gaze cut to me. "I bet you can find an investor if you need one."

"If Misty decides to open a restaurant, I'll be first in line to invest."

Tears welled in her eyes. "You're both very kind."

Randy smiled at her. "We know good cooking and good people when we see them."

"I'll think about it."

I got the feeling when her catering truck was loaded, she'd be glad to see the Fin and Feather in her rearview.

Suddenly restless, I stood. "Thank you for the biscuit, Misty."

"Will I see you at brunch?"

"I'll be there. Also, I meant it about investing. If you ever decide you want a restaurant, let me know. Here. Kansas City. I don't care. I'm in."

"Thank you, Mrs. Jones.

I left Randy and Bear with Misty, walked to Libba's cabin, and knocked on the door.

"Go away!" Her voice was thick with sleep.

I knocked again. "It's me."

"Don't. Care."

"Anarchy is in the hospital."

Two seconds later, the door jerked open. "What?"

"And Buffy Geller is dead."

"Wait. Back up." Libba ran her fingers through her messy hair. "What happened to Anarchy?"

"A copperhead." The snake would feature large in my future nightmares. I had no doubt.

"And he's in the hospital?"

"Yes."

She rubbed her eyes. "What happened to Buffy?"

"Stabbed."

"When?"

"Shortly after four this morning."

She sighed and opened the door wider. "You'd better come in."

I hesitated. "Where's Charlie?"

"Fishing."

I stepped inside, and she pointed at the table. "Sit. I can make coffee."

"I've had enough."

Her brows drew together. "Are you sick?"

"No. I drank a whole pot. Don't look at me like that." Exasperation had claimed her face. "You drink whole pitchers of martinis."

"That's different. Tell me about Anarchy."

"A snake sank its fangs into his wrist." My shudder was soul deep. "He's under observation in intensive care at the county hospital."

"But, he'll be fine."

"What if he's not?" The sorrow and worry I'd bottled up broke through my defenses in an unexpected rush, and I stood in Libba's cabin and sobbed.

She wrapped me in an embrace and let me cry deep, racking sobs.

I soaked Libba's shoulder with my tears. My muscles tensed at the memory of the snake biting Anarchy's wrist. My head ached from stress and adrenalin and worry.

Through it all, Libba rubbed small circles on my back.

I needed to stop. To get ahold of myself. I heard Mother's voice in my head—*Ellison, pull yourself together.*

But reining in my emotions was beyond me. And with Libba, I didn't need to pretend strength. I could show her my weakness and fear and, when I was done sobbing, she'd help me put the pieces back together.

"He'll be fine." Her tone was soothing.

"How do you know?" My voice was a sad plea muffled by her shoulder.

"Because you didn't go through the past year just to lose him. Because you deserve happiness. Because copperhead bites aren't deadly for adults."

I took a shaky breath.

"He'll be fine," she said again.

"You think so?"

"I know so."

Another breath. This one didn't shake. I lifted my head. "I can't lose him."

"You won't." She sounded certain.

I took a tiny step back and looked at her face. She meant what she said.

"Have you talked to him since he went to the hospital?"

"Yes. He said he was fine, but he sounded tired."

"This hasn't been a restful weekend, and he did get bitten by a venomous snake. Of course he's tired." She tilted her head. "Why aren't you with him?"

"I had to make a statement."

"About Buffy?"

"Someone stabbed her in the stomach, and she bled to death."

Libba crossed her arms over her mid-section. "That's awful."

It really was.

"Did Bill kill her?"

"I don't think so. He seemed destroyed when I told him she was gone."

"Then who?"

"She followed him yesterday morning. I think she saw Graham's killer."

"She followed Bill?"

"She thought he might have something going with Misty."

Libba huffed. "Honestly, the woman had sex with her

husband three times a year." She held up three fingers. "His birthday, their anniversary, and one holiday of his choosing. What did she think he'd do?"

"Well, whatever he was doing, it wasn't with Misty."

"Of course not. Misty is young and pretty and too smart to fall for someone like Bill." Libba led me to the table and pushed me onto a chair. "So Buffy snuck around after Bill, saw the killer, then what? Why didn't she say something yesterday? She could have told you. Told Anarchy."

"I don't know."

She joined me at the table. "This weekend would have been fun if Sumner and Graham hadn't come. The man made enemies like Carter makes little liver pills."

"I haven't heard that expression in ages."

"My mother used to say it. Whoever Carter was, he made tons of pills."

"What are liver pills?"

"Laxatives."

"Why would anyone take a laxative for their liver?"

"Don't ask me." She frowned. "We digress. What happens to the investigation with Anarchy in the hospital? Is the cute deputy in charge?"

"Deputy Harden?"

"Tall, tan, shoulders for miles, and a mop of brown hair?"

"That's him. With two murders, and Anarchy in the hospital, the sheriff ought to take charge. In the meantime, Anarchy wants me to observe everyone."

"Is that safe?"

"He wouldn't knowingly put me in danger."

"Hmph. Two people are dead." She reached across the table and clasped my hand. "And you have a way of finding trouble."

She was wrong. Trouble found me.

CHAPTER THIRTEEN

"Would you care for a mimosa?" The server held an array of drinks on a tray covered by a red bandana.

"No, thank you," I replied. Today was not a Champagne kind of day.

"A bloody Mary?"

I shook my head, but Libba picked up a glass and stirred its contents with the celery stalk.

We were gathered beneath the gazebo. Well, most of us. Liz and Willa stood in the corner and talked in hushed tones. Tommy sat at the picnic table with his hand over his eyes. Perry, Thatch, and Fred formed a tight circle nearby. Merit, Charlie, and Mel were missing. I assumed Sumner and Bill weren't coming.

"Is Charlie still fishing?"

"He's taking a shower."

"You didn't wait for him?"

"I wanted a drink." She eyed the picnic table, which was covered in a yellow cloth sprinkled with daisies. "Set for thirteen. Isn't that supposed to be unlucky?"

"Really? You're going there?"

Liz approached us with her hands clasped together. Deep wrinkles cut into her forehead, and she looked decidedly pale. "Good morning."

"Lizzie, are you okay?"

She ran her hand across her face. "Is it true about Buffy?"

"What did you hear?"

"That she's dead." She took a deep, shuddering breath. "That she was murdered."

I nodded. "It's true."

"And Anarchy? What happened to him?"

"He's in the hospital. A snake bite."

"Oh, Ellison. I'm so sorry. Why are you here?" She winced and held her hands up. "That came out wrong. It wasn't meant to be critical. I just mean there must be a really good reason, because I know you, and I know you want to be with him."

"He asked me to stay."

"Here? Why?"

"She's solved murder cases before," said Libba. "Without Anarchy."

Liz wrung her hands. "I wish we'd never planned this weekend."

"You had the best intentions."

"I can't stop thinking about how wrong things have gone. We started as sixteen. Now two people are dead, and one is in the hospital."

Maybe I should have a bloody Mary.

A tall man with gray hair showing beneath his cowboy hat, a mustache drooping beneath his nose, and a star on his chest stepped under the gazebo.

"Liz, Libba, would you please excuse me?" I didn't wait for their responses.

I cut a path to the man and held out my hand. "Sheriff Bascom, I'm Ellison Jones."

He studied me with bright blue eyes.

I studied him, too. For a man in his sixties, he was gorgeous.

"Any updates on your husband, Mrs. Jones?"

"The doctors are keeping him in intensive care, but promise me he'll be fine."

"They see plenty of snake bites. I'd believe them." He took in the small crowd in the gazebo—every member staring at us. "Is there a place we can talk?"

"The clubhouse?"

He nodded his assent, and we walked the path together.

"This is a helluva thing," he said.

"For everyone."

"Does your husband have a lead suspect?"

Perry. "I'm not sure he'd ruled anyone out."

"What about you? Who do you think killed your friends?"

He opened the clubhouse for me, and I led him to Randy's office.

"When it comes to Graham's murder, my thoughts have changed."

"Oh?"

"You may have heard, Buffy, the woman who was killed, lied about her whereabouts yesterday morning."

"I heard."

"It seems likely she saw the killer."

He took off his cowboy hat and put it on Randy's desk. "Agreed."

"I've known Buffy for years, and she wasn't a stupid woman."

He nodded, but said nothing.

"She knew who killed Graham, but didn't say anything. Why not?"

"You tell me."

I sank into one of the comfortable chairs facing Randy's desk. "There are several possibilities. First, blackmail."

"You don't sound convinced of that."

"I'm not. Like I said, she wasn't stupid. If she'd decided on blackmail, she wouldn't have met the killer by herself. Not when everyone else was asleep."

He nodded.

"The second possibility—" I tapped one pointer finger against the other "—she was in league with the killer."

"She killed Landingham?"

"I'm having a hard time seeing Buffy as an accessory to murder, much less an actual killer. Also, if they were in it together, why stab her?" I shook my head. "Graham was a man with many enemies. Buffy was well-liked. I think the third option is most likely."

"Which is?"

"She didn't say anything because she either liked the killer or approved of his actions."

"She condoned murder."

"As I mentioned, Graham had many enemies."

"How does any of that change your mind about who the killer is?"

"Buffy left her cabin in the middle of the night." Willingly, since Bill hadn't known she was gone, hadn't heard a struggle.

"So?"

"She wouldn't do that unless she trusted the killer. Anarchy and I assumed a man killed Graham. Almost every man here had good reason. But I can't imagine Buffy meeting a man in the middle of the night. Not even one she knew. We should have looked harder at the women."

"Any of them have motives?"

"If protecting their husbands counts, all of them do. And there's Merit. She and Graham had an argument Friday night."

"About?"

"I missed the argument. But it must have been passionate. Graham made her cry."

"What about Mrs. Landingham?"

"When I talked to her yesterday, her grief seemed genuine. Since then, I think she's been taking Valium."

"Motive?"

"Anarchy was checking on insurance policies. But unless there's a large one, she was better off with Graham alive."

"Would Buffy have left her cabin to meet Merit?"

"Yes."

"Knowing she was a killer?"

"When you meet Merit, you'll understand. It's hard to imagine her as a threat."

"A wolf in sheep's clothing?" He rubbed his chin. "I spoke with your husband early this morning."

Florence had been willing to put through the sheriff's call, but not mine? She could join Dr. Collins in the nest of copperheads.

"He said you'd agreed to stay here."

"Reluctantly."

"Would you sit in on my interviews?"

I stared at him.

"I don't know these people. You do. You can read their reactions."

I'd promised Anarchy I'd observe. And the faster the sheriff made an arrest or let everyone go home, the faster I could get to my husband. "Fine."

"I noticed most of the people in the gazebo were drinking."

"It's brunch."

"I say we let them drink a bit more."

He was waiting until my friends were tipsy to grill them. With me observing. I crossed my fingers and hoped Mother never found out about this.

"Ellison?" The voice was unmistakable. Had thinking of Mother conjured her from thin air?

A second later, the office door flew open. "There you are.

I've been looking for you." She gave Sheriff Bascom the smallest of glances. "Is this the doltish deputy?"

"No, Mother." I resisted the urge to bury my face in my hands. "This is Sheriff Bascom. Sheriff, meet my mother, Frances Walford."

The sheriff stood, and Mother looked up at him and blushed. Blushed.

He raised a brow. "The doltish deputy?"

"Deputy Kincaid," I replied.

"Ah. Married to the mayor's daughter."

"That explains so much." Not the poor woman's taste, but it did explain how someone like Sheriff Bascom tolerated Deputy Kicked-in-the-Head. The sheriff had no choice. "Mother, I'm delighted to see you." I really wasn't. "But what are you doing here?"

"Grace and I were worried. We drove down."

"Grace is here?"

"She's talking to Libba in the gazebo."

I rose from my chair. "The killer could be in the gazebo."

"Oh?" She lifted her brows. "You're worried about your daughter hanging around a killer? I believe I know how that feels."

Touché. "Grace is a child."

"Libba will keep an eye on her."

Libba was marvelous and funny and naughty and gorgeous and my best friend and the last person on earth who should look after an inquisitive teenager.

I looked at the sheriff. "I need to head back down to brunch."

"I'll join you," said Mother. Then she smiled at the sheriff. "Are you coming with us?" Was she flirting?

"I need to make a call. I'll be down in a few minutes."

We left him in the clubhouse, and Mother said, "Remind me who's on this trip from hell."

"Liz and Perry Brandt."

"Lovely people."

"Willa and Thatch Cooke."

"She's a nice woman."

"Merit and Tommy Dodson."

Her lips pinched. Her nose wrinkled. The expression said far more than words.

"Mel and Fred Paige."

"Have you gone shooting with her? I hear she's very good."

"She is. Libba and Charlie."

"Go on."

"The Gellers."

"Poor Bill."

"The Landinghams."

"What goes around, comes around."

I stopped on the path and stared at her. "What do you mean?"

"He was a horrible man." Mother had no qualms about speaking ill of the dead, not if she thought they deserved it. "He cheated on his first wife with that woman." She paused and shuddered. "Those ridiculous eyelashes. Did she kill him?"

"I think she was better off with him alive."

"You're probably right. Graham spent money like it grew on trees. She needed him alive to make more."

We resumed walking.

"She's here?" Mother pointed at the gazebo. "She's at brunch? Her husband died yesterday."

"Don't point at her."

Mother's hand dropped.

"She's got to eat. And you just finished telling me how horrible Graham was."

Mother sniffed. "That doesn't mean she shouldn't mourn."

"It looks to me like she's mourning." Even from a distance, I could see that Sumner's skin was sallow. Dark smudges marked the skin beneath her eyes. Her hair hung limp. "She looks like ten miles of bad road."

Mother side-eyed me. "You may be right."

"Pardon me. I didn't hear you clearly."

"Don't gloat, Ellison. No one likes gloating."

This from a world-class gloater.

She adjusted her sunglasses. "My money is on Thatch Cooke."

"Why?" I asked.

"I've heard things." Mother could be infuriating.

"What things?"

"He'd do anything to hold on to the managing partner job. Makes me wonder why."

"What do you mean?"

"If I were a partner in that firm, I'd demand an audit."

"Any other suspects?"

"Merit." She tsked. "The whole family is crazy. Her father used to walk around with his suit coat on backward, his arms straight out in front, and groan like Frankenstein's monster. It was unnerving."

"It was Halloween."

"It's still odd behavior for an adult."

"Any other reason you suspect Merit?" I lowered my voice now that we were close enough to be overheard.

"Merit's brother sued over the estate," Mother whispered. "I believe Graham represented him."

"What was at issue?"

"Money. Lots of money. And Merit's brother won."

"No wonder Merit called Graham a money-grubber."

"That woman. She thinks she's better than mere mortals, but she cares about money like the rest of us."

"She had a reason to kill Graham. But Buffy?"

Mother sniffed. "Don't expect me to solve Anarchy's case for him."

"Mom." Grace bowled into me, and I hugged her tightly.

"How's Anarchy?" she demanded. "Have you talked to him?"

"Yes. Thanks to your grandmother, I talked to him a little while ago. He'll be fine."

"A snake." She shuddered. "Did you almost die when it happened?"

"I swear my heart stopped beating."

She grinned. "I bet. Come on." She tugged on my arm. "I'm starving."

We perused the buffet—biscuits, gravy, Misty's homemade strawberry jam, the vegetarian strata she'd mentioned, bacon, fresh fruit, butter-streusel coffee cake, sliced ham, and roasted potatoes.

"This looks marvelous," said Mother. High praise, indeed.

"I had a biscuit earlier. It was heavenly."

We filled our plates and headed to the table, where Misty's staff had added two place settings.

Libba and Charlie sat down across from us, and Mother and Charlie discussed the hospital where Charlie worked and Mother sat on the board. Chaired the board.

Thatch joined us and offered Mother a sunny grin. "Good morning, Mrs. Walford."

Mother acknowledged his greeting with a regal nod. "Good morning."

"Did Charlie tell you the firm will be withdrawing as counsel in Dr. Adams' suit against the hospital?"

Mother's nostrils flared. "I'm surprised anyone in your firm took the case in the first place."

"Graham didn't consult us. He ascertained there was no conflict of interest, then took Adams on as a client."

"That is the bar by which you choose your cases? No conflict of interest?"

Thatch looked mildly panicked, as if he thought he was

wading in shallow water, but suddenly discovered he was swimming in the deep ocean.

I ate my biscuit and enjoyed the show.

"At any rate." Thatch adjusted the collar of his madras shirt. "We're out."

Mother sniffed. "You should never have been in."

Sheriff Bascom appeared, and every person at the table watched him amble closer to us. He gave us an aw-shucks grin, then said, "Mrs. Landingham. I was wondering if I might have a word?"

Across from me, Thatch visibly relaxed.

Sumner stood.

"Mrs. Jones, would you please join us?"

Mother grabbed my arm, leaned forward, and whispered in my ear, "What do you think you're doing?" If only she were as quiet as she thought she was.

"Observing," I whispered back.

"How do get yourself into these messes?"

Everyone was watching us, waiting for me to answer the sheriff's question. Or Mother's.

I offered them a sickly smile, pulled free of Mother's hold, and stood. "Of course, Sheriff."

Sheriff Bascom donned a stern expression and surveyed the table. "I'll need to speak with all of you before anyone can leave."

Thatch grumbled, but Mother silenced him with the lift of an eyebrow.

"If you'll come with me?" Sheriff Bascom directed Sumner and me toward the clubhouse.

"I answered your husband's questions," said Sumner.

"I know it seems excessive, but they're doing their best to find Graham's killer."

She nodded and fell silent.

We entered the clubhouse and settled in Randy's now-familiar office, and Sheriff Bascom asked, "How long were you and Mr. Landingham married?"

"Seven years."

"How did you meet?"

"I was a secretary at his firm."

Sheriff Bascom made a note on a legal pad. "Can you think of anyone who might want to harm your husband?"

Her answering laugh was bitter. "Graham had a knack for making enemies."

"I see. Anyone in particular?"

"No."

"As his widow, you'll inherit his estate?"

"Estate? There's no insurance. I'm left with my jewelry, whatever cash is in our accounts, and a big house with a mortgage I can't afford. Oh, and except for my jewelry, Graham's kids get half."

"No insurance?"

"The firm carried a policy, but we didn't."

"So you don't benefit from his death?"

"The opposite."

"Would you go through your movements yesterday morning?"

"I got up and put on running clothes. I even teased Graham. He'd planned on fishing, but he'd drunk too many cocktails the night prior and was moving slowly."

"And then?"

"Then I went running."

"Did you see anyone?"

"Not until I saw Ellison."

"How far did you run?"

"Around four miles."

"What time did you leave your cabin?"

"Five fifteen."

"Let's go back to who might have wanted your husband dead? Care to elaborate?"

"Everyone here." She glanced my way. "Except for Ellison and her husband."

"Why did you come? It seems odd to want to spend a weekend with people who despise you?"

"Graham never backed down from a fight."

"Where were you this morning between three and four?" The way Sheriff Bascom's questions jumped from topic to topic seemed designed to confuse.

Sumner frowned as if he'd succeeded in befuddling her. "Asleep."

"In your cabin?"

"No. Here in the clubhouse. Our cabin...I couldn't." Tears welled in her eyes. "Not when Graham died there." She lifted her chin. "Not when it's a crime scene."

"Mrs. Geller worked as a nurse before she married?"

"Yes."

"She took care of you yesterday. Did she say anything that might indicate why someone would want her dead?"

"No."

"Nothing?"

Sumner gave a tiny shrug. "She and Bill were having problems." She glanced at me as if she expected me to back her story. "Bill cheated. Often. She was thinking about divorce."

"I see. Did you hear anything untoward last night?"

"Untoward?"

"Someone trying to get into the clubhouse?"

"No. Buffy gave me some pills. I slept like the dead." She winced. "I mean, I didn't hear a sound."

"Thank you, Mrs. Landingham. You've been very helpful."

"That's all?"

"For now."

Sumner left us.

"Is it true?" asked Sheriff Bascom.

"Which part?"

"Graham's estate."

"I can't speak to the insurance, but she's right about the rest. Graham's children with his first wife get half of everything. Roux's divorce settlement may well be the only time Graham lost in court."

"And the Gellers? Was Mrs. Geller considering a divorce?"

"She didn't confide in me, but I wouldn't be surprised."

"What reason did Bill Geller have to want Graham dead?"

"Graham was doing due diligence for a deal—I'm not clear on the details—and discovered accounting irregularities. I think the deal is still moving forward, but the questions raised were awkward."

"How awkward?"

"Mistress on the Country Club Plaza awkward."

"I see. So Mr. Geller appears to have motives for two murders." He stared at the calendar featuring the German shorthair. "I wonder, will anyone else?"

CHAPTER FOURTEEN

*T*hatch leaned back in his chair and steepled his fingers. His gaze traveled Randy's office, and he smirked, as if he found his surroundings and the country sheriff, who dared ask questions, amusing.

Sheriff Bascom mirrored Thatch's movement. He leaned back in Randy's desk chair and steepled his fingers. Unlike Thatch, he didn't smirk. "I understand you're an attorney, Mr. Cooke."

"Yes." Thatch stretched out his legs, and his smirk deepened. Being polite, being helpful, being concerned—all options. Instead, Thatch was behaving like an arrogant ass. He was an arrogant ass, but usually he was smart enough to hide it. Why not make the effort with the sheriff?

"You were partners with the deceased, Mr. Landingham?"

"Yes."

"How did you know Buffy Geller?"

"She and my wife are—were—friends."

I clasped my hands in my lap and tried not to think of Buffy's lifeless body, or the utter lack of concern in Thatch's voice.

"Do you often spend weekends away with your wife's friends?" asked the sheriff.

"No. But Willa and Liz thought this would be fun." Thatch offered a women-there's-no-pleasing-them shrug.

"Who decided who'd be invited?"

"Willa and Liz." Thatch glanced my way. "Who asked you, Ellison?"

"Liz." Although it was Libba who'd pressured me to come.

Thatch grinned as if I'd proved his point. "Eight couples, with the cost of the weekend split eight ways."

Sheriff Bascom tilted his head. "The cost?

"Extra staff at the club, the caterer, the cabin rentals."

"I see. Why come here?"

Thatch tilted his head. "What do you mean?"

"It's the hottest time of year. Your wife could easily have planned a weekend at the Lake of the Ozarks."

The sheriff made an excellent point. If we'd gone to the lake, we could have gone waterskiing or tubing. The fishing would be better, and I was certain we could have found a stable for those who wanted to ride.

"You'd have to ask her."

"It seems to me she selected a remote location." Sheriff Bascom glanced at me. "When did Mrs. Brandt invite you and Detective Jones?"

"Liz called me Tuesday morning." Tuesday. And we'd arrived on Friday. The weekend wasn't a sudden whim. The catering, the staff, readying the cabins—they'd required planning. With all that work, Liz and Willa would have filled the eight cabins long before Tuesday. "I think there was a cancellation. Anarchy and I were a last-minute addition."

"Is that true, Mr. Cooke?"

The smirk was back. "You'd have to ask my wife."

Sheriff Bascom nodded as if he planned on doing just that. "Were you and Graham Landingham friends?"

"We worked together."

A small frown pulled at the sheriff's lips. "That doesn't answer my question."

"No. We weren't friends."

Sheriff Bascom frowned as if Thatch's answer confused him. "But your wife put the weekend together?"

"Yes. With Liz."

"Then why did they include Sumner and Graham Landingham?"

Thatch shifted in his chair. "Graham and I were colleagues. It was important for us to get along."

"And you thought a weekend in the country would help with that?"

"It couldn't hurt."

"Except Mr. Landingham is dead."

"Are you suggesting I killed him?" Thatch's tone was itching for a fight.

"I'm not suggesting anything." The sheriff's reply was mild. "Where were you early this morning?"

Thatch rolled his shoulders. "Asleep in my cabin with my wife."

"No insomnia?"

"No. I slept like a baby."

"You didn't hear the commotion when my deputies and the ambulance arrived?"

"I'm a deep sleeper."

"What will happen to Mr. Landingham's clients?"

"Other partners will take them on, or we'll withdraw as counsel."

"Did the firm carry a life insurance policy on Mr. Landingham?"

If I hadn't been watching, I'd have missed the sudden stiffening in Thatch's shoulders, there and gone in a flash.

"We have policies for all our partners," he replied.

"How much was Mr. Landingham insured for?"

"Five million dollars."

Wow. My jaw dropped. That was five times what I expected.

"To be paid to the firm, not Mrs. Landingham?"

"That's right."

"Does the firm carry policies in that amount on all its partners?"

Thatch's lips pinched, and he rubbed a hand over his face and smoothed his features. "Graham made a lot of money for the firm."

"That doesn't answer my question, Mr. Cooke."

"Policy benefits range from a hundred thousand to five million." He sounded as if the topic bored him.

"How many partners are insured for five million?"

"Three. Graham, Perry, and Gregory Frasier."

"Have you always carried such large policies?"

"No." Thatch's response was grudging.

"When did the policies go in force?"

Thatch looked the sheriff in the eye. "Six weeks ago."

"I see." The sheriff nodded as if Thatch had confirmed a suspicion. "Fortuitous timing. Was Mr. Landingham well liked among his colleagues?"

"He'll be missed for his financial contributions to the firm."

"I'll take that as a 'no.' I believe he was trying to unseat you as managing partner."

"Is that a question?"

"More of an observation. Would he have succeeded?"

Thatch stretched his legs to impossible lengths. "No."

"You sound very certain."

"I am."

Sheriff Bascom tapped the tips of his fingers together. "Who benefited from Mr. Landingham's death?"

"His wife, I suppose."

"She did not. Mr. Landingham was worth far more to her alive. His death will be a financial blow."

Thatch frowned as if he'd received bad news.

"The five million dollars from the insurance policy, that will be divided among the partners?"

"Yes."

"Equally?"

Thatch schooled his features into a neutral mask. "No."

"As managing partner, will you receive a larger share?"

"There's a formula. It's complicated." The subtext was loud— the formula was too complicated for a rustic sheriff.

"Make it simple for me, Mr. Cooke. How much will you receive?"

"Between a quarter of a million and three-hundred thousand."

"I see." The sheriff rubbed his chin. "I recently read that the median salary in the United States is around fifteen thousand dollars a year. You'll receive up to twenty times that. Seems to me you had a motive."

Thatch let several seconds tick by. "Perry Brandt. One of Graham's largest clients will revert to Perry. Perry benefits more than anyone."

It had taken less than fifteen minutes for Thatch to offer his friend as a suspect.

"Reverts?" asked the sheriff.

"Perry brought the client, a tobacco company, into the firm. Then Graham wooed them."

"I imagine that caused hard feelings?"

"Yes."

Sheriff Bascom nodded, as if Thatch had given him the answer he wanted. "Will Mr. Brandt receive part of the proceeds from the firm's policy on Mr. Landingham?"

"Yes."

"How much?"

"There's a formula."

"Yes, yes. The formula. Venture a guess."

"Two hundred thousand."

"I see." He sat straighter in his chair. "This has been helpful. Thank you for your time, Mr. Cooke."

Thatch rose from his chair, but before he reached the door, Sheriff Bascom said, "One more question, Mr. Cooke."

"What is it?" Thatch didn't try to hide his annoyance.

"Does the firm carry a policy on your life?"

"I told you. We carry policies on all the partners."

"For how much is your life insured?"

A flush darkened Thatch's cheeks. "A hundred thousand."

Sheriff Bascom allowed himself a smile. "Thank you, Mr. Cooke. That will be all."

Without a word, Thatch left.

The sheriff let a few seconds pass, then stood and went to the door. He poked his head out and nodded.

Bear took the opportunity to squeeze past him.

"Hey, buddy." I held out my hand.

His furry bod wriggled in anticipation of scratches, and he trotted to my side.

As soon as I touched his ears, his tail wagged.

Sheriff Bascom watched me pet Bear. "What are your impressions?"

"Thatch was posturing."

"Agreed."

"He's worried. He had two reasons to kill Graham. The money and protecting his job as managing partner."

Sheriff Bascom nodded.

"Do you think Thatch and Willa planned Graham's murder?" I asked.

"Mrs. Cooke seems like a very nice lady."

"Not an answer."

"I think it's possible. You're the one who said Buffy wouldn't leave the safety of her cabin to meet a man. Would she leave to meet Willa? Or Liz?"

Liz? My heart stopped as I thought of her appearance at brunch. The woman who was always perfectly poised had seemed distracted. Had she felt guilty? No. I refused to believe that. Liz would never commit murder. Never. "You suspect them because they planned the weekend?"

"Would you invite someone you can't stand to spend the weekend with you?"

I thought of Prudence Davies and her horse teeth and her barely contained disdain for me. I'd do a lot to avoid spending a weekend with her. "No," I replied. "I wouldn't."

"You see why I suspect them?"

"I do. But if Liz and Perry were planning to murder Graham this weekend, why would they ask a homicide detective to join them?"

Sheriff Bascom rubbed his chin. "An excellent question. Can you find the answer?"

Could I question my friend? I glanced at the phone. "If you don't mind, I'll check on my husband first."

He chuckled. "I'm sure whoever answers will put through your call immediately."

"You heard about that."

"Your mother has friends in high places."

"It's best not to cross her."

"She must be very proud of you."

"I think mostly she wishes I wouldn't find bodies."

"You can't blame her for that. How would you feel if you daughter found bodies?"

"I wouldn't hold it against her."

He chuckled again and left me.

The operator put through my call immediately.

"Hello." Anarchy sounded stronger. Still tired, but stronger.

"It's good to hear your voice." I couldn't keep the smile off my face if I tried.

"Yours too."

"How are you feeling?"

"Fine."

Fine. He'd been bitten by a venomous snake. There was no way he felt fine. He was hiding something from me. Well, I had a secret of my own. "I have a surprise for you."

"You caught the killer?"

"No." I took a breath. "Mother and Grace are on their way to see you."

"What?" His voice boomed through the phone. "Now? Why?"

"They came to the club. But Mother needs doctors to bully, and I don't want Grace anywhere near whoever killed Graham and Buffy."

"So you sent them to me?"

"I'll worry less if I know Mother is watching over you." If there was any issue with his health, she'd wear down the doctors until it was solved.

"She'll terrify the staff."

"They might discharge you sooner."

"Don't pretend there's a bright side."

"I love you."

He huffed. "You're lucky you're fabulous."

"Am I?"

"You are. And I love you, too."

I paused in front of Liz and Perry's cabin door and collected my thoughts. It wasn't as if I could come right out and ask her if Willa and Thatch had killed Graham and Buffy.

This conversation needed delicacy and finesse. I was in short supply of both.

A twig snapped behind me, and I glanced over my shoulder.

Merit, who came from the direction of Sumner's cabin, gave me a half-hearted wave, and asked, "Do you know when the sheriff might let us leave?"

"He's interviewing the staff now."

"We can leave when he's done?"

"He may have follow up questions. "

She sighed her frustration. "This whole situation has been awful. We never should have come."

"Why did you?"

She stared at me.

"It doesn't seem as if you enjoy our company."

"You gossip."

"Everyone gossips."

"I don't."

"You can tell yourself that—"

"Because it's true! You're an artist, not some pandering prole. You should be above wagging your tongue."

"Like you?"

She lifted her nose in the air.

"I want to know if someone's daughter is getting married or having a baby. I can throw a shower. I want to know if someone is sick. I can send flowers or soup or the latest bestseller. I want to know if someone is having difficulties. I can be there for them." Or ask Aggie to bake a Bundt cake.

"You make gossip sound benign. What about cheating spouses?"

"Believe me, I know all about cheating spouses. And I'm sure everyone and their brother discussed my marriage with Henry."

"That didn't bother you?"

"I didn't love it, but I didn't think less of anyone for talking."

"Saint Ellison. Not all of us feel that way." Then, realizing she'd revealed too much, she marched toward her own cabin.

I lifted my hand to knock on Liz's door, but she opened it.

"I heard you talking to Merit." She took a step back. "Come in."

I stepped inside. The cabin smelled of Liz's perfume and was impossibly tidy.

Liz went to the bed, where a stack of neatly folded clothes sat next to an open suitcase.

She saw me looking, and said "Perry says the sheriff can't keep us here. We're driving home this afternoon."

"It's been a rough weekend."

Her expression softened. "Especially for you. How's Anarchy?"

"Mother's on her way to the hospital."

"You're worried about him?"

My throat tightened, so I nodded.

"She'll have the whole hospital jumping whenever she says, 'boo.' He'll get the best care in the world."

"I hope so."

"You didn't come to talk about Anarchy."

"No. May I ask you a few questions?"

"As a friend, or as homicide detective's wife?"

I thought before I answered. "As a friend."

"Go ahead."

"Who was supposed to come this weekend?"

"What do you mean?"

"Were Anarchy and I a late addition?"

"We were thrilled you could come." Of course she was gracious and polite.

"We were thrilled to be asked. On Tuesday. Who bowed out?"

"Rosalind and Gregory Frasier. Rosalind's mother fell and they needed to stay with her."

"Whose idea was it to invite us?"

"Mine."

"Did you check with Willa first?"

She frowned. "No. But why would Willa care? She adores you."

Adores me? That was a stretch.

Someone had plotted a murder and seen it through despite the presence of a homicide detective. That spoke of desperation.

"Who decided to invite Sumner and Graham?"

"Thatch wanted them here."

"Thatch says you and Willa invited them."

She flushed, and covered her cheeks with her palms.

"What is it, Liz?"

"It doesn't reflect well on Willa. Or me."

I waited.

"Graham was a horrible man. He stole Perry's biggest client and he decided to run for managing partner just to unnerve Thatch."

"So you invited him on a weekend trip?"

"Graham had an affair."

"Buffy told me. Some woman at the firm."

"No."

"Then who?"

"Misty."

I stared at her. "Misty, the pretty-young-caterer Misty?"

"We wanted him to know that if he messed with our lives, we'd mess with his."

"Does Sumner know about her?"

"No. We're not monsters."

"You're sure she doesn't know?"

"Positive."

"What about Misty? Did she know Graham would be here?" I didn't need Liz's confirmation. "She made his favorite dessert."

"What are you talking about?"

"Pineapple upside-down cake. It was Graham's favorite. Misty served it Friday night."

Liz refolded a perfectly folded shirt. "It wasn't kind of us.

And I'm not proud of what we did, but we didn't kill Graham. Or Buffy."

"Thatch and Perry knew your plan?"

"Not Perry. I didn't tell him. He doesn't know about Misty. And he has too much integrity to…" her voice petered out.

She thought Perry had too much integrity to hire Graham's mistress as a caterer when it might hurt Sumner. I didn't say that. "How did you find out about Graham and Misty?"

"Thatch told Willa."

"How did Thatch know?"

"Every Thursday afternoon, Graham left work early. Thatch got curious and had him followed."

Graham was an unpleasant man. Thatch wasn't much better. He might be worse. It seemed entirely possible that he'd killed Graham, then roped Willa into killing Buffy.

Liz put the shirt she'd folded three times now into the suitcase. "What now?"

"I honestly don't know." The murders and the snake bite and the lies were all muddled in my head.

"Perry will be disappointed. In me." Her gaze held a plea.

She wasn't worried about the sheriff or his suspicions. She worried about her husband's good opinion.

"He's a smart man. He might already suspect."

"Suspecting and knowing are very different things."

She was right. "I'll try to keep this quiet. But if it has anything to do with the murders…"

"I understand." She hugged me. "Thank you."

"I'll let you finish packing." As I walked away, our conversation niggled at me. I'd missed something. I was sure of it.

CHAPTER FIFTEEN

For the first time this weekend, the heat didn't bother me. Inside, I was so cold, the soaring temperature couldn't touch me.

I trudged to the gazebo, collapsed onto a bench at the deserted picnic table, and thought about Willa Cooke.

Had she lured Buffy to her death? Had she been the one to slide the knife into Buffy's stomach?

The first tendrils of a headache sprouted in my brain. I couldn't think about Willa. I couldn't.

Instead, I put myself in Buffy's shoes on the morning of Graham's murder.

As Bill left, she'd slipped out of bed, pulled on clothes and boots (because she was as afraid of snakes as I was), and followed him.

She'd watched as he made his way to the clubhouse.

That much I knew. What then?

Had she hidden in the shadows in case he turned around?

Had the sweet morning air smelled bitter? Had she startled at each sound?

I bet she hated sneaking after him. Maybe even hated herself for doing it.

Bill hadn't stayed long in the clubhouse. A few minutes. Just enough time to exchange a few words with Misty and a fill a thermos with coffee.

Then what? Had Buffy breathed a relieved sigh when her husband emerged so quickly?

What had she thought as she followed him back to their cabin, where he'd found her missing?

Why hadn't she stepped forward? Was she too embarrassed to admit she'd followed him?

I dropped my head into my hands.

At what point did she notice someone else lurking in the darkness?

If I spotted someone lurking in the dark, my heart rate would spike and my mouth would go dry. I'd be ready to run. But Buffy hadn't run—at least not the Buffy of my imagination.

Had she worried it might be one of her friends on their way to meet Bill?

Had she recognized Thatch? Or was it someone else?

Had I walked past Buffy in my search for coffee?

If only she'd spoken up—told Anarchy or me who she saw—she'd be alive.

"Mind if I join you?"

I looked up at Perry. "I can't promise you good company."

"Likewise." He sat across from me. "You were deep in thought."

"There's a lot to think about."

His usually sparkling eyes were serious, and the expression on his face was grim. "I'm not sorry Graham is dead."

Not what I expected him to say. "You had good reason to wish him ill."

He rubbed the back of his neck. "I did. I knew we weren't

friends, but we were partners. I thought we could trust each other. Then—"

"Then you picked my wedding reception over a business trip. For what it's worth, I'm glad you and Liz were there."

He nodded. Slowly. "Is she a suspect?"

"Liz?" He'd surprised me again. "As far as the sheriff is concerned, everyone's a suspect."

"And you? What do you think?"

"Liz is innocent. She'd never hurt anyone."

"You don't need to convince me."

I managed a weak smile. "I cleared you, Liz, Libba and Charlie immediately."

"Despite our motives?"

"I know you. I know Liz. Lord knows, I know Libba. And, despite Libba's track record of picking terrible men, Charlie's a good one. None of you are killers."

"That leaves you with plenty of suspects."

It did. "Mother said something to me early today. It's been bothering me."

"What did she say?"

"If she were a partner in your firm, she'd demand an audit."

Perry's grim expression turned stony. "That's one of the reasons Graham wanted to be managing partner. So he could order an audit."

"He suspected Thatch was embezzling?"

Perry rubbed his neck again. "Thatch would never break the law."

That was wishful thinking.

I suspected there were few lines Thatch wouldn't cross. "It's a good reason for Thatch to want Graham dead." And that didn't touch on the insurance money. "Tell me about the life insurance policies the firm carries on the partners."

"How do you know about those?"

"Humor me."

"It's a common business practice."

I lifted my brows.

Perry huffed his displeasure. "Fine. The policies were Thatch's idea."

Of course they were. "The amount seems excessive."

"A million dollars?"

"A million?" I shook my head. "Thatch told the sheriff that you, Gregory Frasier, and Graham were insured for five million. Each."

For a long second, Perry didn't move. Didn't react. "I must have misunderstood."

"A four-million-dollar misunderstanding?" That seemed highly unlikely.

"We approved a budget for insurance. Maybe he got a deal on the premiums and could afford more coverage."

More wishful thinking.

The headache bloomed inside my skull. "Do you think he might have killed Graham?"

"Of course not." Perry was a loyal friend. Better than Thatch deserved.

I wasn't nearly as convinced. It was too easy to imagine Thatch shooting Graham. "Then who?"

"I don't know. I sat at the brunch table earlier today and wondered who among us was the killer. I could hardly eat." He offered me a rueful smile. "And Misty's food is always amazing."

Misty. I should have found her immediately after I talked to Liz. I stood. "Perry, would you please excuse me?"

"Did you figure something out?" He rose from the bench.

"I don't know. Maybe."

He looked curious, as if he wanted an explanation.

But I wouldn't betray Liz's trust, not if I didn't have to. "I'll talk to you later."

I hurried to the clubhouse kitchen, where I found Misty scrubbing the porcelain sink with Comet and a yellow sponge.

"Good afternoon, Mrs. Jones." She turned on the tap and rinsed.

"Where is your staff?" They ought to be helping her.

"They left within thirty seconds of the sheriff giving his permission. Not that I blame them."

Nor did I. They hadn't hired on for a weekend of murder. "Do you have a moment?"

"I'm almost done cleaning. Is there something wrong?" She squeezed the sponge, tossed it into the sink, and faced me.

"I wouldn't ask, but two people are dead."

She gave me an I'm-well-aware look and leaned against the counter.

Sweat trickled between my breasts and beaded at my hairline. Was there a tactful way to ask?

Misty tilted her head. "What's your question?"

"You and Graham Landingham?"

She didn't move. Not a muscle. Then she found a fascinating spot on the ceiling and stared at it. "What do you mean?"

"You had a relationship?"

Her eyes filled with tears, but she said nothing. Instead, she stared at the ceiling as if her life depended on it. Long seconds passed.

I wiped the sweat from my brow and waited.

Finally, she nodded. "How did you find out?"

"Does it matter?"

"No." She shook her head. "I don't suppose it does."

"For how long?"

"Two years. We met at the firm. There was an attraction, then a friendship. It wasn't something we planned. It just happened."

"You knew he was married?"

She flushed. "Yes. They weren't happy."

"He told you that?"

"He didn't have to." She looked me in the eye. "Happily married men don't cheat."

Unhappily married women still cared when their husbands wandered. I had first-hand experience.

"Graham and Sumner went to counseling because Graham had an affair. Presumably with you. Did you stop, then pick up again?"

The color on her cheeks deepened. "We never stopped."

Poor Sumner. She'd gone to counseling to save her marriage and her husband hadn't even given up his girlfriend.

"You're young and smart and pretty. Why Graham?" She could do better than a middle-aged man with thinning hair, a thickened waist, and a wife.

"He didn't make demands. Try telling a man you can't go out with him on weekends because you work Friday and Saturdays. Tell him you can't spend the night because you have to get up at five and prepare breakfast for fifty. Most of the time, I smell like onions or garlic or sugar. Graham didn't care. We met on Thursdays, spent the afternoon together, had dinner, and went our separate ways until the next Thursday rolled around. Easy. Uncomplicated." She rested her hand on her belly.

The gesture was gentle, even tender.

Oh dear Lord.

Pain pulsed behind my eyes as I remembered an earlier conversation. "Randy said this was a great place to raise a family."

Her lips thinned.

"Are you pregnant?" Because being pregnant with a married man's baby seemed pretty darned complicated to me. And that was before he was murdered.

Her chin barely moved, but she definitely nodded.

"Did Graham know about the baby?"

Another tiny nod. "I told him Friday night. I haven't felt well, and I missed our last few Thursdays. He wanted to know why."

"How did he react?"

She crossed her arms over her chest. "I didn't want anything from him. I told him I could support this child without his help." She shook her head. "I guess I don't have a choice now."

"What did he say?"

"He said the baby was a miracle. He wanted to be part of his or her life. He said he wanted to do it right this time." She tucked a loose strand of hair behind her ear. "He and his children don't have the best relationship."

Because he'd dumped their mother for Sumner. "Did you love him?"

"I liked him. He was funny and smart and interested in me and my business."

"How did Randy find out?"

She sighed. "Apparently, he peeked into the kitchen on Saturday morning when I wasn't here. Yesterday afternoon, he asked me where I was, and I told him."

"Where were you?"

"Sometimes the food smells get to me. I was in the bathroom."

I leaned against the kitchen table and pressed my fingers to my temples. "Who do you think killed Graham?"

"Look, Mrs. Jones, you've been really nice to me, but—"

"You liked him well enough to cry over his death."

She shook her head.

"Your child's father."

She tilted her chin and looked at the ceiling again. "I don't have any proof."

"Who?"

"Thatch Cooke."

"Why?"

"Mrs. Cooke is a nice woman."

"I agree. But you can't let her husband get away with murder because you like her."

She sighed. "Graham was sure Mr. Cooke was embezzling. But revealing that would have caused a huge scandal. He was trying to force Mr. Cooke out of the firm."

"By challenging him for the managing partner job?"

"Graham would have won." Her smile was cynical. "The fix was in."

And Thatch's motives to kill Graham kept getting stronger.

"Does anyone else know about the baby?"

"No."

"What about your affair with Graham?"

She shrugged. "I'm not even sure how you know."

And I wasn't going to tell her. "You're sure Sumner didn't know the affair was ongoing?"

"Her friends wouldn't have hired me to cater this weekend if she knew."

But Graham knew. And Graham would have understood the implicit threat.

I glanced around the kitchen. "Are you leaving soon?"

"The sheriff said I could go whenever I like. When I finish cleaning the kitchen, I'll hit the road." The kitchen still needed work. Milk crates filled with pots and pans still littered the counters. The floor needed sweeping, then mopping. And the top of the six-burner stove needed to meet Misty's sponge. She reached up and tightened her ponytail.

It was a gesture I saw from Grace at least once a day, and it reminded me that Misty was young.

She had told Graham she didn't need his help with the baby. But she didn't know how hard motherhood could be. The sleepless nights, the spit up, the diapers, the worry over tiny rashes, the bone-deep exhaustion.

And that was just the first week.

"I meant what I said about the restaurant. If you need an investor, let me know. The hours might be better than catering, especially for a new mother."

She offered me a tiny smile. "Thank you, Mrs. Jones. I'll keep that in mind."

I found Willa sitting on a blanket in the shade by the lake. She wore a linen shift and sandals and she'd French braided her hair, then tucked the tail. She looked like a fashion model waiting for a photographer. Cool and elegant and composed.

Especially when compared to me. Hot. Sweaty. Tired.

"Willa?"

She shifted her gaze from the water and nodded. Once. As if she expected me. "Liz said she spoke with you."

"We talked. "

She patted the blanket. "You'd better sit. Explaining how we could be so awful will take time."

I dropped onto the blanket next to her. "Graham was awful." Not that his behavior excused theirs. Poor Sumner.

"It's no excuse."

"One thing is bothering me."

She loosed a bitter little laugh. "Just one?"

"If you wanted to cause trouble for Graham, why not just tell Sumner about his affair with Misty?"

Willa resumed staring at the water.

I studied her expression. Her forehead creased. Her lips thinned. Her brows drew together. "You did tell her."

She nodded. "Not my finest moment."

"How did she react?"

"Sumner started out as the other woman. She knew she couldn't trust her husband before she married him." Willa twisted her torso and looked me in the eye. "His affair with Misty couldn't have come as a surprise."

"How did she react?"

"She went still, then her face turned red. For a moment I

thought she might cry or throw a glass of water in my face—we were at Nabil's. She didn't."

"What did she do?"

"She asked for a name. When I wouldn't give it to her, she pretended not to care. That's when I knew how badly I'd hurt her." Willa's shoulders slumped. "It was wrong of me. Unforgivable, really. I shouldn't have hurt Sumner to get back at Graham."

"Liz doesn't know you told Sumner?"

"No. If Liz knew, she'd have found another caterer for the weekend. She's not cruel."

"That's not a word I'd have used to describe you, either." Vain, elegant, willowy, and slightly scattered, but not cruel. "Why didn't you hire a different caterer?"

"Thatch insisted on Misty." She sighed. "It's funny, the things we'll do for those we love. I always thought I was a good person. Now, look at me. I hurt someone. And for what? Thatch's office politics?"

She turned and stared at the lake.

I stared at her profile.

Neither of us spoke, each lost in her own thoughts.

Maybe Willa was thinking about Thatch.

I was thinking about office politics. Was that what the kids were calling embezzlement these days? More likely, Willa didn't know about the embezzling or the insurance or Graham's efforts to have Thatch removed from the firm.

Well, I wasn't going to be the one to tell her.

"I think we can safely say this is the worst weekend away ever. Ever. I don't think I'll ever plan another."

As terrible as she'd found the past few days, I could guarantee that Bill and Sumner thought they were worse. "Maybe the memory will fade."

"Do you think she'll ever forgive me?"

"Sumner?"

"Mhmm."

"Of course." A lie. One that didn't matter. Willa might attend Graham's funeral, but after that she'd never see Sumner again. Sumner would disappear from our lives. She'd been included because of Graham. Without him, she'd slip away.

"I went to their wedding. Sumner was so in love, so hopeful. She had the man she loved, and she wanted a family. She was determined to have three children—two boys and a girl. She looked so young and blissfully happy. I almost forgot she was the other woman."

A light breeze ruffled our hair as I thought of Sumner standing at an altar with Graham.

Willa stretched her legs and crossed her ankles. "Any idea when the sheriff will let us go home?

"I suspect it will be late this afternoon."

She snorted. Even her snorts were elegant. "You suspect, or you know?"

I froze.

"Ellison, what's wrong?"

"Something Liz said. 'Suspecting and knowing are very different things.'"

"That's obvious. Why would that bother you?"

It bothered me because I'd missed something and needed to reconsider who might have killed Graham and Buffy. It bothered because it meant there was still someone in danger.

I scrambled off the blanket and took off at a dead run.

CHAPTER SIXTEEN

I ran.

The soles of my cowboy boots bit into the gravel on the path.

My feet flew.

My arms and legs pumped.

My breath came in short rasps.

The sun beat down on me as if it had made melting me into a puddle of goo its personal mission.

I promised myself a swim in a pool large enough to hold cool water. I promised myself arctic air-conditioning. I promised myself a gallon of iced tea mixed with lemonade.

And I kept running.

I reached the clubhouse, more sweat than woman, and threw open the door.

Bear, who was sprawled in front of the cold fireplace, lifted his head and wagged his tail. Had I come to pet him?

I had not. I dashed into the kitchen.

Misty had made progress. Every surface sparkled, and the stove was so clean it looked brand new.

Only three milk crates filled with cooking equipment remained.

The caterer was gone.

"Misty?"

No one answered.

Dread, dark and heavy, stole what little breath I had left.

I hurried through the kitchen to the short hallway that led to the pantry. The empty pantry.

"Misty?" Between the breathlessness from my sprint and dread, my voice was barely a whisper.

I trotted back to the kitchen. Where was she?

One of the milk crates, the blue one, lifted a supercilious brow. "Did the heat melt your brain?"

Quite possibly. Especially if milk crates were talking to me.

"The last time you burst in here, there were seven of us," said the blue crate.

"Cut her some slack," said the yellow crate. "She looks exhausted. Hot. Tired."

And I had a terrible headache.

The blue crate huffed. "She looks like a dirty, wet dishrag, one that needs to be thrown away. And she smells awful. Worse than sour milk."

"You would know," said the red crate.

"Like your milk has never gone bad," the blue crate replied.

"Don't listen to them," said the yellow crate. "They get like this when they're tired. Misty went outside a few minutes ago."

I nodded my thanks and opened the back door. The sun reflecting off Misty's white van nearly blinded me, and I squinted.

The yellow crate was right. Misty was outside. She stood beside the open door to her van with hands in the air. Tears ran down her pretty face.

Too bad the yellow crate hadn't warned me about the woman with the 12-gauge shotgun.

For a half-second, the cicadas' drone filled my entire head. Their song drowned out my headache and my panic, but not the sound of the blue crate saying, "I told you the heat melted her brain. She knew Sumner was the killer, knew she might target Misty, and still ran out there without a weapon."

The blue crate had an attitude problem.

The blue crate was also right.

Sumner's back was to me. Maybe I could sneak up on her. Tackle her. Struggle for the gun.

Not the smartest plan. Not even close. But being beyond hot, beyond sweaty, beyond sleep deprived, and possibly dehydrated didn't leave much brain power for rescue plans.

"Mrs. Jones," said Misty. "Please, help me."

So much for the element of surprise.

Sumner swung around and pointed the shotgun at me.

I held up my hands. "Sumner, you don't want to do this. Put down the gun."

"You shouldn't have come up here, Ellison."

Arguably, she was right. But running into situations without considering consequences wasn't new behavior. Next time, I'd find a detective or sheriff before I went rushing in. Where was the sheriff? "Sumner—"

"Move!" She jerked the shotgun barrel in Misty's direction. "Over there."

Staring down a shotgun barrel was my new least favorite thing. "Sumner—"

"Are you deaf?"

"You can't kill us."

She glanced at the gun in her hands. "I can."

"Why?"

She jerked her chin in Misty's direction. "She doesn't get to have it all."

"She won't. Graham is gone."

"Her fault," said the woman who'd killed Graham.

I needed time. Time for Randy or the sheriff or someone to find us. I had to keep her talking.

"Did you plan Graham's murder?"

"No. But Friday night changed everything. Move."

I shifted a few steps. "You realized Graham was having an affair."

"Graham was always having an affair." Sumner's upper lip curled. "But he met someone. He changed."

"You knew it was Misty?"

"No. But it wasn't hard to figure out. She's his type."

Both Sumner and Misty were pretty blondes with big blue eyes.

"He watched her. Every move she made. I thought he'd hit on her. I didn't realize they already knew each other, not until she said she'd baked Graham's favorite dessert."

"Pineapple upside-down cake."

"That's right. She made his favorite. Now, move."

I took another tiny step. Misty and I were harder to kill when we were separated.

Sweat ran into my eyes, and I blinked away the sting. "That must have been awful for you."

"You want to know the awful part?" Her expression darkened. "I thought Willa and Liz were my friends. But they asked Graham's chickee—" Sumner pointed the shotgun at Misty "when they knew I'd be here."

"Liz didn't know about Misty."

"As if I'd believe you."

What had I ever done?

Whatever it was, Sumner didn't appreciate it. Once again, she pointed the shotgun at me.

I swallowed. *Keep her talking.* Hope someone comes. "You stole Perry's gun to kill Graham?"

"Actually, no. Liz mentioned the gun at dinner, and I was so furious with her for inviting Misty that I decided to take it. I stole the gun to cause trouble. To make the Brandts worry." She rolled her neck. "When the party ended, Graham and I went back to our cabin. He claimed he'd forgotten his glasses at the gazebo. I knew better. He left them on purpose, so he'd have a reason to go back and talk to her." She shifted the gun's barrel to Misty.

She'd been holding the gun for long minutes. Was it getting heavy?

I didn't notice a shotgun's weight when I was shooting, but to simply stand and hold one? I'd get tired.

Then again, Sumner had adrenalin and a healthy dose of crazy fueling her.

"I followed him and heard what she told him. She's pregnant. With Graham's baby. He knew I wanted children. More than anything. I begged. I pleaded. I even tried to trick him. But no baby. Not for me. Then he knocks up a caterer? A caterer named Misty. With a name like that, she should have been a stripper."

"It wasn't on purpose," said Misty.

"Shut up!" Sumner pointed the barrel at Misty's chest.

Misty really needed to keep quiet.

"Sumner, please, don't do this. You don't want to hurt anyone else."

"What would you know?"

"Henry cheated on me. He made me a laughingstock. He slept with Prudence Davies." I'd have rather he slept with ten caterers than with her.

Sumner lowered the gun. Slightly.

Encouraged, I continued. "He slept with Kitty Ballew and Madeline Harper and—"

"Did he rub his indiscretions in your face?"

"All the time."

The gun dropped another inch. "What did you do?"

"I counted the days until I could file for divorce."

"What stopped you?"

"We agreed to wait until Grace was out of high school."

"Your daughter."

"Yes."

"I don't have a daughter." She lifted the gun's barrel.

"I'm sorry." Misty's face was red, and her eyes were puffy. "I never meant to hurt you."

Sumner's eyes narrowed.

"Then what?" I shouted to get Sumner's attention. "What did Misty say about the baby?"

"She told Graham she didn't want him involved. But he wouldn't listen. He started talking about private nursery schools and putting money aside so her bastard could attend his alma mater. That's when I decided to kill him."

But not in the heat of the moment. She'd waited until the next morning to shoot her husband in the chest. Then she'd pulled on her sneakers and gone for a run.

"You were smart. We didn't suspect you. Why did you plant the gun in Mel and Fred's cabin?"

"That was a mistake. I meant to hide it in Willa and Thatch's cabin. Graham hated Thatch, and Willa invited her." She nodded toward Misty. "But I heard someone on the path, so I ducked into the closest cabin."

"Buffy knew?"

"She did. She saw me on Saturday morning and guessed what I'd done."

"She kept your secret."

"She understood about cheating husbands. Bill can't keep it in his pants." Sumner chuckled. "I bet she wanted to kill him at least three times a week."

"Then why kill her?"

"What if she changed her mind? I couldn't take that risk. I convinced her to meet me at the cabin. I told her I felt guilty and wanted to talk about turning myself in."

"You stole one of Misty's knives."

"I was staying in a room at the clubhouse, so I cut through the kitchen and took a knife. Easy-peasy."

Sumner was sort of terrifying.

"You stabbed her."

"I did." She frowned. "She stood there with a shocked look on her face, as if she couldn't believe I'd done it. Then she ran. She went crashing into the woods, calling your name. I tried to follow her, but I heard you and your husband. I had no gun, no knife. I couldn't stop her from telling you everything. Couldn't stop you from calling the authorities." She gave me a triumphant smile. "But she died."

Sumner was definitely terrifying and definitely several marbles short of a full bag.

Keep her talking.

"Ellison." The back door opened, and Merit stuck her head out. "There you are. I need to speak with you."

How had she missed Sumner and the shotgun?

Bear squeezed by her and raced to my side.

"Ugh. Now I have dog hair on my pants."

She might be the single most unobservant woman on the planet.

"At any rate, I came to apologize. I shouldn't have called you a pandering prole."

"Merit, run."

She stood there and stared at me.

Why didn't the blue crate insult Merit? Her behavior was more stupid than mine.

Sumner swung the gun away from Misty, away from me, and pointed the barrel at the back door.

"Sumner, what are you doing?" Merit's voice was sharp. "You'll shoot someone."

Blue crate? I waited for a snarky remark, but the blue crate remained silent.

I returned to my original—my only—plan.

I ran at Sumner, wrapped my arms around her waist, and tackled her to the ground in a cloud of choking dust.

The shotgun blast was deafening, and my head threatened to split in two. Like Zeus's, but without birthing Athena.

Sumner struggled. Hard.

I reared up, brought back my arm, and hit her as hard as I could. The impact traveled from my fist to my shoulder, and my knuckles screamed in pain.

In a perfect world, Sumner would have gone limp or passed out or cried, "Uncle."

The world wasn't perfect. Not even close.

Sumner slapped me.

She spit.

She curled her fingers into talons and clawed at my skin.

I coughed on the thick dust as sweat poured down my forehead and into my eyes.

Bear joined the melee.

He barked.

He snapped.

He closed his jaws around the gun and dragged it from Sumner's hands.

Sumner's hand met my cheek in another slap, and the sting brought tears to my eyes.

My fist met her nose and something—cartilage or bone—cracked. Blood covered her face, and my hand, and our chests.

If Mother could only see me now.

A hand closed around my upper arm, but I wrenched free.

"Easy, Ellison," said Sheriff Bascom. "It's me."

The fight drained out of me and I slumped to the ground. Or, more accurately, the dirt.

"Are you hurt?" he demanded.

"Sumner confessed. She killed them both."

"Are you hurt?" he repeated.

"I'm not sure." I turned toward the van. "Where's Misty?"

"She's fine, but her van will need a new tire."

"Mrs. Jones." Randy lifted me off the ground. "Let me help you. Let's get you inside, get you a cool drink."

"And aspirin?"

He frowned his concern. "Did you hit your head?

"My headache started before the fight."

"I'll get you aspirin," he promised. Then he led me inside.

I collapsed onto a chair and rested my aching head on the kitchen table.

Bear sat next to me and rested his chin on my lap.

"Here." Randy pressed a glass into my hand. "Drink slowly."

"Look who's back," said the blue crate. "You didn't die. Surprise, surprise."

I narrowed my eyes and glared at the blue crate. He deserved dirty looks. He was a jerk.

"Mrs. Jones?"

I lifted my head.

"You need to drink."

I took a sip of ice water. It tasted like ambrosia.

"Slowly," Randy warned. "I think you might be dehydrated."

I was definitely dehydrated. It was the only explanation for the talking crates. "What's happening outside?"

He glanced out the window. "Deputy Harden is putting Mrs. Landingham in the back of a squad car. The sheriff is talking to Misty."

"You're sure she wasn't hurt? The gun went off."

"She's fine."

"What about Merit?"

"Merit?"

"Yes, Merit. Mrs. Dodson."

He gave me a blank look.

"She was in the kitchen."

He frowned. "Let me get you those aspirin."

"She let Bear out."

Hearing his name, Bear wagged his tail.

Randy reached into a cabinet, pulled out a bottle, and shook two pills into his hand.

He handed them to me, and I swallowed them with the last of my water.

"More?"

"Please." I handed him the empty glass, then stroked Bear's head. "This is one fabulous dog you have."

"Don't I know it."

"What happened to Merit?"

"She wasn't here when we arrived."

"She didn't go for help?"

"We came running when we heard the shotgun."

I rubbed my temples, and Bear nudged me. If I rubbed anyone's temples, they should be his.

"I have a dog at home," I told him. "He's brave like you, Bear. His name is Max." I leaned down and brushed my lips across Bear's fur. "Don't tell him I told you, but you're much better behaved."

Randy grinned. "He's got you snowed."

"He's a hero. And you haven't met Max. Max is on a mission to conquer the world. Bear just wants a comfy place to nap."

The back door opened, and we both turned.

Sheriff Bascom stepped inside and took off his hat. "How are you feeling, Mrs. Jones?"

"Better. Thank you for asking."

"We need to talk." He rubbed his neck. "Would you like to shower first?"

I was covered in sweat and blood and dust. In fact, the dust had adhered to the sweat and blood, and my skin tone varied from dirty brown to sickly gray. "That would be nice." More than nice, being clean would be better than coffee. I stood and swayed.

Randy caught my elbow. "Use my bathroom."

"Pardon?"

"If you don't mind my saying, you look shaky. I'll go to your cabin and grab clothes for you. You stay inside in the air-conditioning."

The thought of walking to the cabin was daunting. Also, I wasn't sure I wanted to be alone. "Thank you."

He led me to his small apartment, and I hardly noticed the aged leather furniture or the hunting prints on the wall. I was too focused on the tiny bathroom with its tiny shower stall. I set the water temperature to tepid, then climbed in.

The Fin and Feather was close enough to Paola to have actual water lines, which was a blessing. Because I lingered in the shower long enough to empty a cistern. Randy favored gold Dial soap and Body on Tap shampoo (which according to the label was one-third beer), and when I finally wrapped myself in a bath towel the unfamiliar scents clung to me.

The mirror above the sink showed me a woman with bags beneath her eyes, but at least the sweat and dirt and blood were gone. Also, the aspirin was kicking in, and my headache had retreated from DEFCON 2 to bearable. Things were looking up.

"Ellison?" Libba's voice came from the other side of the bathroom door. "I brought you clothes."

I opened the door, and she frowned at me. "Wow. You look awful."

"Thanks."

"Here." She thrust clean underwear and a sundress at me. "Get dressed, then we'll talk."

Two minutes later, I emerged from the bathroom and found her waiting.

"Do you have a brush?"

"Sorry. I'm not carrying a purse."

My hair could stay a rat's nest, at least it was clean.

"Talk," she demanded.

"Sumner did it."

"That's it? That's all you're going to say?"

"I don't have the energy for much more, and the sheriff wants to talk with me."

"Willa told me you took off running." Her eyes narrowed. "That means you figured out that Sumner was guilty and ran toward danger."

I shrugged.

"We'll put aside the running-toward-danger bit. For now. How did you know it was Sumner?"

"There's a difference between suspecting and knowing."

"What's that supposed to mean?"

"Can I explain later?"

Libba crossed her arms and scowled at me.

"Between the heat and the adrenalin and the fight—"

"The fight?"

I held up my hand and let her see my bruised knuckles. "The fight."

She grinned. "You hit Sumner? I'm so jealous. Also, when you mention fighting, waiting for an explanation gets less and less attractive."

"Too bad."

"Charlie needs to check you out."

"Charlie is a cardiologist."

"Which means he's smart enough to tend to your cuts and bruises and make sure you're not concussed."

"I need to talk to Anarchy."

"I'll make a deal with you. Let Charlie check you out, then we'll drive you to the hospital."

"I have to talk to Sheriff Bascom."

"Let Charlie check for head injuries, then talk to the sheriff. Then we'll take you to Anarchy."

How could I refuse an offer like that? "Deal."

CHAPTER SEVENTEEN

We crowded into Anarchy hospital room—me, Libba, and Charlie.

Anarchy looked pale.

Pale enough to make me worry. "The doctor is sure you'll be okay?"

"Positive." I wanted to believe him, but he was a man. And in my experience, men acted like head colds were the bubonic plague, while treating serious illnesses like paper cuts.

"Charlie, what do you think?"

"I'm a cardiologist."

"Who examined me for a concussion."

He grimaced as if he regretted shining a flashlight into my eyes. "You need to trust Anarchy's doctors."

Anarchy nodded. "Frances has them so frightened, they get out the defibrillator paddles when I sneeze. I'm getting the best possible care."

"Where is Mother?"

"She took Grace to get something to eat. Now—" he nodded toward an empty chair "—sit and tell me what happened with Sumner."

"Ellison was in a fight," said Libba. "A real roll-in-the-dust, throw-punches-that-split-her-knuckles, fist fight."

"Ellison!"

My shoulders tensed at Mother's appalled tone. Apparently, she and Grace were back.

"How could you?"

"The alternative was getting blown to smithereens with a 12-gauge shotgun." I regretted those words when I saw Grace's eyes widen.

Mother looked down her nose. "The whole story. I want the whole story." She frowned at Libba and Charlie, who stood, then at me. I'd had the audacity to take the only seat in the room. "We need more chairs."

She stepped into the hallway, and within seconds, orderlies carried additional chairs into Anarchy's room.

Satisfied that everyone had a place to sit, she inclined her chin at me and said, "You may begin."

"I don't know where to start."

"With the fight," said Libba.

"The fight comes at the end," I replied.

Anarchy reached for my unbruised hand and gave it a gentle squeeze. "How did you know it was Sumner?"

"Liz said suspecting and knowing weren't the same things, and the idea rattled around my brain."

"That's how you figured it out?" Libba rolled her eyes. "You could have just as easily thrown darts. I was certain Thatch killed Graham."

"I thought so, too. For a while. He had so many reasons to want Graham dead. Also, I didn't see how it could be Sumner. She was better off with Graham alive."

"And what Liz said changed your mind?" Anarchy stared at me as if he were trying to figure out exactly how my brain worked.

"Not exactly, but it did make me think. Sumner knew

Graham had affairs. That was nothing new. They'd even been to marital counseling. She suspected the woman he was seeing might be different—a real threat to her marriage—but she didn't know. Not until Friday night."

"What happened Friday night?" asked Grace.

"Sumner realized Misty was the other woman."

Anarchy rubbed a small circle on the back of my hand. "How?"

"Misty made Graham's favorite dessert. It somehow tipped off Sumner to their relationship. So, later, when Graham snuck back to the gazebo to talk to Misty, Sumner followed him and eavesdropped. She heard Misty tell Graham that she was pregnant."

"She can't be very far along," said Charlie. "The woman's got a great figure."

Libba flicked him in the center of his forehead.

He clasped a hand to his head. "Ouch!"

"Keep your eyes to yourself."

"Children." Mother's voice held a warning.

"The one thing Sumner wanted, the one thing Graham refused to give her, was a baby."

"And he got his mistress pregnant." Charlie shook his head. "I bet she was livid."

"Mad enough to kill," I agreed. "She used the gun she'd stolen from the Brandts to shoot Graham."

"How long was Graham dead before you found him?" asked Charlie.

"He was still warm," Anarchy replied.

Mother's cheeks went pale.

Charlie shook his head. "She was cold-hearted enough to shoot her husband, then go for a run?"

"Yes. And she took the gun with her. Buffy saw her with it."

"Buffy saw her?" Libba's brows rose. "She swore to me she was asleep in her cabin."

"She lied. She followed Bill to make sure he didn't have an assignation with Misty."

"Misty gets around," said Mother.

"There was nothing between Misty and Bill." Misty wasn't blameless, but she had not taken multiple lovers.

"Let's get to the fight," said Libba.

"Hold your horses. Where was I?"

"Buffy followed Bill," said Anarchy.

"May we come in?" Liz stood in the doorway with Perry, who held an enormous floral arrangement.

Mother looked with approval at Liz's ensemble—linen pants and a white camp shirt paired with low-heeled sandals and a Gucci shoulder bag. Then her gaze swung my way. I wore a wrinkled sundress with cowboy boots, and my hair was caught in a messy bun.

I swallowed, looked down at my boots, and noticed the toe was dotted with blood.

"Sit," Mother insisted. "I'll arrange for more chairs."

When the orderlies brought more chairs, and everyone was seated, there was no room to move.

"Ellison," said Mother. "You may continue."

"Ellison was just telling us why Sumner killed Graham and Buffy." Libba grinned at Liz. "Apparently, you gave her the clue."

"Me?"

"Something about knowing and suspecting," Libba replied.

Liz frowned in confusion.

"Never mind, Liz. I was just saying Buffy followed Bill and saw Sumner."

"Who had my gun?" Trust the lawyer to follow the thread.

"Yes."

"Wait a minute." Charlie held up his hand. "Why didn't Buffy tell Anarchy she'd seen Sumner?"

"The fool woman might be alive if she had," said Mother.

"Buffy had a certain amount of sympathy for Sumner's role as a wronged wife."

"The fight," said Libba.

"What is it with you and the fight?" I asked.

"It's just so out of character. I have to know more."

"Fine. When I figured out Sumner was the killer, I worried she might hurt Misty, so I went to the kitchen." I sounded blasé about a run that had left me panting.

"Was she there?" asked Grace.

"No, but I looked outside." I refused to mention the talking crates. "And I spotted her by her van. Sumner had a shotgun pointed at her."

"Where on earth did she get a shotgun?" asked Mother.

"I assume the range, but Randy has a collection in the clubhouse. Regardless, where she got it, it was a 12-gauge."

"That could do some damage," said Charlie.

"Go on, Ellison," Mother instructed.

"I tried to keep Sumner talking in hopes Randy or Sheriff Bascom would come."

"What happened?" asked Liz.

"Merit opened the back door."

"Merit? Merit Dobson?" Mother wrinkled her nose. "What did she want?"

"She wanted to apologize for calling me a pandering prole."

"A what?" Mother was outraged.

"A pandering prole."

"There is nothing proletariat about you."

Anarchy's lips quirked. And I had to look away from his handsome face to keep from laughing.

"Get to the fight," said Libba.

"Right. Merit let Bear out, and Sumner was distracted, so I rushed her."

"Pardon me." Mother's brows lifted. "What did you say?"

"I rushed her, Mother. I ran at her and tackled her to the ground."

"Good heavens." Mother pressed a manicured hand to her chest. "Whatever gave you that idea?"

"I didn't want to die."

Grace grinned at me. "I think it's cool, Mom. You saved that woman."

"Thank you, honey."

Mother wore a thunderous expression. "That ghastly Landingham woman might have shot you."

"Sumner gave every indication that she'd shoot me if I didn't do something."

"So you tackled her." Libba rolled her hand in a circle for me to keep the story rolling. "Then what?"

The gun went off. I kept that part to myself. "I hit her."

Libba sighed. "I wish I could've seen that. Give me details."

I stared at my best friend. "I hit her, then Bear jumped in."

"Who is Bear?" asked Mother.

"Randy's dog. The black lab. Bear pulled the gun from Sumner's hands. Then, Sheriff Bascom and Randy arrived."

Mother pressed a palm to her forehead. "You're so very lucky. No one was injured?"

"Just my knuckles." I held them out so she could admire the bruises. "Oh, and I broke Sumner's nose."

Mother gasped.

"Oh, come on, Frances," said Libba, who must have been feeling exceptionally brave. "The woman had it coming. She stole Perry's gun, killed two people, nearly killed Ellison, and ruined my weekend."

"What will happen to her now?" asked Liz.

"She was arrested and booked on two counts of first-degree murder," I replied.

"Which means she'll be in jail for a long time," said Perry.

Anarchy yawned.

Mother stood. "Everyone out."

We stared at her.

"I mean it. The doctor says it's important for Anarchy to rest." Within thirty seconds, she had the room cleared. "Ellison, you may stay."

Gee, thanks.

Without another word, she took her leave.

Anarchy smiled at me. "Busy day."

"Yes."

"You promised to be careful."

"I did."

"Tackling a murderer doesn't strike me as careful."

"I didn't have a better choice."

He shifted to the left side of the bed and patted the mattress.

"What will the doctors say?" I was fairly certain doctors frowned on visitors climbing into bed with their patients.

"Nothing. Frances has taken away their ability to say anything except, 'yes, ma'am.'"

I climbed into the bed with my husband and rested my head on his shoulder.

He stroked my messy hair, and I snuggled closer.

I breathed him in. He might be tired, but he was whole and healthy. Only the bandage on his wrist and the paleness of his cheeks suggested he'd had a run-in with a snake. "Our next vacation, we're going somewhere far away. No one we know. No one who speaks English."

He chuckled. "You mean you didn't have fun?"

"Fun?" I'd melted in the heat. Found two dead bodies. Been insulted by a crate. And ended up rolling in the dust with a murderer. "Are you kidding?"

The door opened, and Perry stuck his head through. "Sorry to interrupt, but I wanted to invite Anarchy to our Thursday card game." He looked over his shoulder as if he worried Mother would catch him disturbing us and snatch him bald-headed. "It's a friendly game." He winced. "Actually, it's not that friendly. Larry plays like the fate of the world depends on him winning. And Dan chews on a cigar and eggs him on."

I strongly suspected Dan was not alone in that.

"Insults are thrown. Bourbon is consumed. And everyone has fun. Except for Larry. You'd think someone who likes to win as much as he does would learn the rules. Can you come?" He looked at Anarchy expectantly.

"I'd like that."

"Great. Seven o'clock. The men's grill at the club. See you there." He glanced again over his shoulder, then stepped into the room. "I have to know. Did you ever suspect me?"

"Not for a moment," I replied.

Perry directed a devilish grin at Anarchy and raised a questioning brow.

"What Ellison said."

"Uhuh." His grin widened. "You might want to work on that poker face before Thursday."

I couldn't let him leave. Not yet. "Perry, what Mother said about Thatch? She's seldom wrong."

"Already taken care of. But thank you for caring. You're a good friend." He winked, then withdrew before Mother could catch him.

"What did I get myself into with this card game?"

"No idea. Women aren't allowed. Perry likes you." As far as I knew, no new players had been added to the Thursday night group in years.

"I'm a likable guy."

I tilted my head and kissed his jaw. "Yes, you are." I'd worried about Anarchy fitting into my world. Seemed like he was doing just fine.

"What were we talking about before Perry came in?"

"Fun weekends. Which this was not."

"Before that?"

"What your doctor would say if he found me in your bed."

"Before that?"

"I don't recall." I would not incriminate myself.

"I told you to be careful."

"You told me to ask questions, and that's what I did."

He chuckled. "I believe I told you to ask questions and observe. Tackling a woman holding a shotgun is not observing. It's acting."

"She was going to kill us both." Just thinking about it made my shoulders tighten.

"Are you okay?"

"Fine." I held up my bruised hand, and he kissed it.

"I don't mean your knuckles. I mean you." Concern darkened his eyes. "Are you okay?"

"I was terrified." My voice was small.

"There would be something wrong if you weren't. Most people, when they're scared, they freeze. You act. It's the definition of bravery."

"I think Mother would call that stupidity."

"Potato. Potahto."

I poked him in the ribs.

"Hey, now."

"Do you ever feel like you're missing out by not having children?" I asked.

The wattage of his smile dimmed. "We talked about this before we got married. I have you. I have Grace. That's all the family I need."

"I don't want you to have regrets." Sumner had committed murder over her regrets.

He caught my chin between his fingers and tilted my head until I looked into his coffee brown eyes. "You're beautiful and brave and kind and I love you. No regrets. Ever."

"You say that now, but you haven't spent the Christmas holidays with Mother." She was so invested in making sure every-thing was perfect that she drove everyone crazy.

His answering laugh rumbled through me. "You are it for me."

I smiled at him. "I feel the same way."

His lips moved closer to mine. "Then we have nothing left to talk about."

There was magic between us. I felt its heat burn from my toes to the top of my head. "Stop talking and kiss me."

And that's what he did.

ALSO BY JULIE MULHERN

The Country Club Murders

The Deep End

Guaranteed to Bleed

Clouds in My Coffee

Send in the Clowns

Watching the Detectives

Cold as Ice

Shadow Dancing

Back Stabbers

Telephone Line

Stayin' Alive

Killer Queen

Night Moves

Lyin' Eyes

Evil Woman

Big Shot

Fire and Rain

The Poppy Fields Adventures

Fields' Guide to Abduction

Fields' Guide to Assassins

Fields' Guide to Voodoo

Fields' Guide to Fog

Fields' Guide to Pharaohs

Fields' Guide to Dirty Money

Fields' Guide to Smuggling

Bayou Series

Bayou Moon

Bayou Nights

Printed in the USA
CPSIA information can be obtained
at www.ICGtesting.com
CBHW050723190224
4401CB00083B/865